Books by T.A. Chase

Dracul's Revenge

I0684298

Dracul's Blood
Anarchy in Blood

The Four Horsemen

Pestilence
War
Famine
Death
Peace

The Beasor Chronicles

Gypsies
Tramps

Home

No Going Home
Home of His Own
Wishing for a Home
Leaving Home
Home Sweet Home

International Men of Sports

A Sticky Wicket in Bollywood
Chasing the King of the Mountains
At First Touch
Blindsided
Burning Up the Ice

Serving Love at Carnival
A Grand Prix Romance
An Ace in the Tiebreak

Rags to Riches

Remove the Empty Spaces
Close the Distance
Following His Footsteps
Anywhere Tequila Flows
Walking in the Rain
Barefoot Dancing

Delarosa Secrets

Borderline
Snap Decision
Cold Truth

The Blood & Thorn Ranch

Bulls and Blood

Merging Violently

Fall into My Kiss

Every Shattered Dream

Every Shattered Dream: Part One
Every Shattered Dream: Part Two
Every Shattered Dream: Part Three
Every Shattered Dream: Part Four
Every Shattered Dream: Part Five

Sexy Snax

Two for One

Where the Devil Dances

What's His Passion?

Mountains to Climb
Climbing the Savage Mountain

Anthologies

Unconventional at Best
Unconventional in Atlanta
Semper Fidelis
An Unconventional Chicago
Unconventional in San Diego
Aim High
Unconventional in Kansas City

Single Titles

Out of Light into Darkness
The Haunting of St. Xavier
From Slavery to Freedom
The Vanguard
Ninja Cupcakes
Stealing Life
Lassoes and Lust
His Last Client
No Bravery
Always Ready
Possibilities
Ajay's Birthday Gift
The Unicorn Said Yes
Hearts on the Line
Voice for the Silent
Threadbare Gypsy Souls

Threadbare Gypsy Souls

ISBN # 978-1-78686-066-8

©Copyright T.A. Chase 2016

Cover Art by Posh Gosh ©Copyright 2016

Interior text design by Claire Siemaszkiewicz

Pride Publishing

Published in 2016 by Pride Publishing, Newland House, The Point, Weaver Road, Lincoln, LN6 3QN, United Kingdom.

Pride Publishing is a subsidiary of Totally Entwined Group Limited.

THREADBARE GYPSY SOULS

T.A. CHASE

Dedication

Thank you for sticking with me through all the years.

Chapter One

The roar of a powerful engine drew everyone's attention on that fine spring day in Fallen Creek, Wyoming. The town was way off the beaten track, so visitors were rare, and no one remembered any other citizen from the area having a car that sounded like that.

Windows rattled and people stopped what they were doing to watch the big motorcycle rumble down Main Street. The rider was hidden behind a black helmet and leathers. One concerned townsperson called the sheriff, alerting him to the invasion of their town, like he hadn't heard the noise.

By the time the bike stopped in front of The Watering Hole, Fallen Creek's most popular bar, the sheriff was there, waiting. He studied the man, who climbed off the bike and stretched. He spied the small wince as the stranger removed his helmet.

"I should've known there'd be a welcoming committee at some point," the blond man drawled as he nodded toward the sheriff.

"We don't get many visitors, son, and it's not like you snuck in or anything like that. Your bike there could wake up the dead around here." Sheriff Carter gestured in the direction of the Harley.

"True. It's better to get this over with right away, anyway. Instead of letting it fester until you arrest me for something stupid." The man set his helmet on the seat before stripping off his leather jacket.

Again, Carter noticed a grimace of pain, and he wondered what kind of injuries the newest arrival to Fallen Creek had and how he'd gotten them. He straightened from where he leaned against his truck when the man approached.

"Here's my wallet. It's got my license in it, and I'm sure you'll want to run it. My name is Nash Rhodes, and while I got into some trouble a while back, I'm not going to cause any around here." Nash held out a black leather wallet that looked hand-tooled and had a skull etched into it.

Carter took it and glanced at the skull. He'd seen something like that before but couldn't remember where. It would come to him eventually. He flipped open the wallet, ignored the large wad of money it held, and looked at Rhodes' license.

His name was Nashville Rocky Rhodes. Carter winced. "Hell of a name to saddle a kid with," he commented.

"Mom has a wicked sense of humor," Nash said, sounding like it was something he was used to talking about.

"I guess so."

Rhodes was from Nashville, Tennessee, and had hit his thirty-second birthday a week ago. Reading Nashville jarred another hidden memory, and Carter knew he'd be heading back to the office to find out why. It might have something to do with the police reports he'd been going over earlier that morning.

"You're a long way from home, Rhodes."

Carter handed back the wallet and propped his hands on his hips. Nash stuffed it into the back pocket of his jeans. He held himself stiffly, making Carter wonder if Nash expected trouble, or if he was in pain.

"Yes, sir. Heading out to Santa Monica. My mom lives out there, and I decided to take a road trip to visit her."

Nash pressed his hand against his left ribs, and the sheriff determined that was one injury, but he had the feeling there were others. He wouldn't be surprised to find out Nash was only a week or two out of the hospital.

"And you aren't planning on causing any problems while you're here?" Carter asked.

Nash's laugh was cut short, and he braced his hand on

Carter's truck. "Do your best to trust me, Sheriff Carter. I don't plan on doing anything except relaxing and resting for a week or two before I continue on. I thought I'd be able to basically drive straight through, but all those months in the hospital drained my reserves, I guess."

"What were you doing in the hospital?"

Shaking his head, Nash smiled. "You can find out on your own, Sheriff. I'm going to go get a drink and something to eat. After which, I'm going to find a room to crash in for a while."

"Sounds like a good idea. Did your doctors talk to you about taking it easy for a while? Seems like you've had some rough times lately." Carter studied Nash, seeing the flash of annoyance in the man's eyes.

Nash stood straight and held out his hand. "It was nice meeting you, Sheriff. I'm sure I'll be seeing you around town."

They shook hands, and Carter watched the man stroll into The Watering Hole. After the door shut behind him, the sheriff climbed into his truck and headed back to his office.

Nash walked away from the window, where he'd been making sure the sheriff was leaving. Once he was gone, Nash went to the bar and sat, leaning his elbows on the bar top and taking a deep breath.

"What's your poison?"

He looked up to see a tall redhead smiling at him. She was around fifty, and there was something about her that reminded him of his mother.

"I'd like a beer and a glass of water, please."

With the medication he was on, he probably shouldn't be drinking, but one beer shouldn't cause a problem. He didn't plan on driving any time soon. He needed to rest because every part of his body ached.

His doctors had protested his leaving, but he'd needed to get out of Nashville before he got sucked back into the club.

After they'd released him from the hospital, he'd taken a few minutes to throw some clothes into his saddlebags, then he'd taken off. He didn't want to see anyone from the club until he'd straightened out his path. Two hours out of Nashville and he'd known it wasn't the best idea he'd ever had.

"You look like ten miles of bad road, mister." She set the glasses in front of him and smiled. "Are you sure you should be out and about?"

Nash chuckled. "Probably not, ma'am, but I've never been good at listening to authority figures."

"You remind me of several guys I've known, and none of them took orders well either. I'm Jeanette and I own this place."

"Good to meet you, ma'am. It's a nice place." Nash glanced around, finishing his glass of water in a few gulps.

He was telling the truth. The Watering Hole might have been a bar, but it wasn't a dive like some of the places Nash had hung out at in Nashville. Those businesses were dark and smelled of sweat, smoke and fear. Jeanette's place was airy and gave off a feeling of welcome, like he could spend several hours there without worrying about catching some kind of disease.

"Thanks. It serves its purpose." She nodded at the beer. "Flag me down if you want another."

"Yes, ma'am."

He sipped the beer and sighed. It wasn't his drink of choice, but he'd learned the hard way that whiskey did bad things to his judgment. So he'd stick to beer and maybe manage to keep out of trouble for a while.

Nash was working on finishing his beer when the door slammed open and a man almost fell into the bar, catching himself at the last moment. He braced his hand against the doorframe and stared over at Jeanette, his bleary eyes trying to focus.

"Well, it's about time you showed up, you no-good, drunken idiot." Jeanette propped her hands on her hips and glared at the stranger.

"Shut up, woman. I'm here now."

Nash turned and leaned his elbows on the bar, watching as the man staggered across the floor to a stool. He collapsed onto it and rested his head on his hands.

"Why don't you get me some food and water, woman? Instead of harping at me all the time."

Jeanette huffed and, with anger and finality clear in her voice, she said, "You're done, Clay. I told you the last time this happened, I wasn't dealing with your drunkenness and your rude-ass attitude. I'm running a business here, and you not showing up for work doesn't help me."

"Shut up, bitch. You're not going to fire me. There isn't anyone else to do the work, and Robinson won't be happy if you let me go," Clay growled at Jeanette.

"Maybe I'll have to work twenty-four-seven, but you know what? I'd rather work myself into the grave than deal with you any longer. Get out of here, Clay, and I don't want to see you in here until you've dealt with your problems."

Nash tensed as Jeanette came around the bar and approached Clay. He could tell the man wasn't going to go without a fight, and Nash couldn't let Jeanette bear the brunt of the man's anger. Pushing to his feet, he knew he was going to regret his chivalry, but his mom hadn't raised him to ignore a damsel in distress.

Before he could say anything, Jeanette reached out to grab Clay's arm, and Clay swung around, backhanding her. Nash rushed across the floor and caught the man's wrist as he was swinging again.

Jeanette touched the red mark on her cheek and snarled, "I'm calling Carter and telling him to throw your ass in jail, Clay. Being Robinson's brother isn't going to get you out of this. I won't tolerate being hit."

"Try it," Nash warned Clay when he struggled to get free. "I'll let a lot of things slide, but laying hands on a woman isn't one of them."

"Fuck you, asshole. Do you know who I am?"

Clay's spittle hit Nash in the face, and he grimaced. Christ, the man smelled like he'd been on a week-long binge without showering. Nash looked over at Jeanette.

"Where do you want me to put him until the sheriff comes?"

Jeanette motioned for him to let Clay go. "He's drunker than a skunk, honey. He won't be any trouble, no matter how badass he thinks he is. Just keep an eye on him for me."

"Certainly, ma'am."

Nash let go of Clay, shoving him a little. He grinned as Clay pin-wheeled his arms to keep from falling over. Folding his arms over his chest, Nash spread his legs slightly and waited.

He'd been around men like Clay all his life and he knew the drunk wouldn't let a slight to his manhood go. Little did Clay know that Nash had been the sergeant-at-arms for his club and had dealt with men far bigger than Clay.

Of course, he regretted everything he'd done as the enforcer for the gang, and he no longer got any enjoyment out of fighting or hurting others. Still, he wasn't going to let Clay disrespect Jeanette again.

Clay telegraphed his punch and Nash easily dodged it. He threw his first punch, pulling his power somewhat. He felt the bones of Clay's nose crunch under his knuckles. Clay's head snapped back and blood splattered over their shirts and the floor.

Surprise slowed him down a little when Clay shook off the blow and came after him again. Most of the men Nash had hit like that would've been down for the count, and he hadn't hit the man with all his power.

"Clay Turner, you stop right there. Don't you go after that man," Jeanette yelled from behind the bar.

"Fuck you, Jeanette, and fuck this asshole. Who does he think he is? Hitting me and thinking he won't get his ass handed to him."

Clay dove at him, and Nash went down, hitting his head

on the floor. As he shook off the stars, Clay nailed him in the ribs. Pain shot through Nash and he roared, putting his hands in the middle of Clay's chest and throwing the man halfway across the room.

"Who taught you manners? You don't talk to a lady like that," Nash yelled as he came to his feet.

"Jeanette ain't a lady. She's just some bitch who thinks she's better than other people." Clay spat in Jeanette's direction.

While Clay was distracted, Nash raced forward and wrapped his hand around Clay's throat. He tightened his grip, lifting the man off the floor and shaking him.

"She is better than you, that's for sure. Now apologize to her before I rip your head from your shoulders. I've fucking reached the end of my patience." Nash bared his teeth at Clay.

Nash almost dropped the man when Clay went limp. Had Clay passed out or something? Nash checked, and Clay peered down at him with a rather submissive expression on his face. He gave the drunk another hard shake before setting him on his feet.

"What do you want me to do with him, Jeanette?" He didn't take his gaze off Clay. He didn't trust the sudden change of attitude from the man.

"Clay, sit your ass at that table and stay there. Carter's on his way to get you."

"Ah, Jeanette, you know I didn't mean anything by it. I'd never hurt you," Clay whined.

Nash snorted, while Jeanette rolled her eyes.

"I've heard that lie too many times, and not just from you, Clay. I'm done with your attitude and your drinking." Jeanette waved Nash back to the bar. "I owe you another drink, son."

He took a breath and his entire body screamed from the pain. He ground his teeth together to keep from yelling. Nash grabbed the edge of the bar, gripping it so tight he thought he might break it.

Jeanette stared at him, worry clear in her eyes, but she didn't say anything. He was glad about that. No point in letting Clay know Nash was injured.

"I'll take a rain check on the drink, Jeanette, though I'd love a glass of water." Nash turned his back to Clay and dug his bottle of painkillers out of his jacket pocket. He shook one out, popping it into his mouth before putting the medicine back.

"Here you go. Why don't you sit? I'd like to talk to you about taking Clay's job." Jeanette set the glass in front of Nash.

He picked it up and swallowed the pill, along with some water. After finishing, he handed the cup to her.

"I'm not staying here long. Just taking a break for a while, then I'll be moving on," he warned her.

"That's all right. I can probably find someone to take your place when you're ready to leave. I just don't have time to find anyone who'll stand up to Robinson at the moment." Jeanette shook her head. "Bastard's got the entire town scared."

"Even the sheriff?"

Carter hadn't struck Nash as being a guy who backed down from bullies, but he was new in town, so what the hell did he know?

"Carter tries, but with no one to back him, it's a little difficult to get anything done." Jeanette folded her arms over her ample bosom and glared at Clay. "Robinson and that pack he runs with have been ruling things for a while here."

Nash snorted. He knew all about gangs. Most tended to be full of bullies trying to gain power through hurting those weaker than them. For most of his life, he'd been one of them, but his time in the hospital had got him thinking about where his life was headed.

"I can't give you any references," he admitted. "There are a lot of people back home I don't want to know where I am."

"Fine with me." Jeanette didn't seem concerned about his past.

"And I'll be honest with you because I know the sheriff will probably be telling you all about it soon enough, especially when he finds out you hired me. I've been in and out of jail since I was sixteen. Mostly assault charges. I've never stolen from anyone and I don't plan on doing it now." Nash rubbed his fingers over the letters etched into the top of the bar.

He could feel Jeanette studying him. He'd done everything he could think of to erase any clue to his having been in a motorcycle club. His cuts were stuffed in his saddlebags, and he didn't plan to wear them anymore. The leathers he wore were plain black, without any sign of what club he'd been affiliated with. It would keep him from getting his ass handed to him while he traveled.

"You were part of the inner circle?"

Startled, he tensed. "What makes you think I was part of a club?"

"You weren't just part of a club. I'm betting you were in a trusted position." Jeanette flashed a small grin. "I've seen a lot of bikers come and go over the years. You've got the look of being in charge. No one in a club gets like that unless he's part of the inner circle."

Nodding, Nash met her gaze. "I was the sergeant-at-arms. I'm not proud of what I've done, but I'll own up to it. No one's to blame for my past except me, and I'm the one who has to deal with it when the time comes."

"True, but as long as you're not looking to cause trouble here, I don't have a problem with what you did before. Also, it'll help if things get out of hand around here. I have a couple of guys bouncing for me, but once in a while, they need help."

The door opened and Nash turned to see Carter stroll in, an annoyed look on his face. Jeanette pointed at Clay, who had napkins pressed against his nose to stop the bleeding.

"He started it," she said.

Carter glanced over at Nash and commented, "And I suppose you finished it?"

Nash shrugged but didn't take his gaze from away from the sheriff. "I'm not looking for trouble, but I'll be damned if anyone is getting hit in my presence."

"Clay hit you?" Carter stepped toward Jeanette, concern clear on his face.

Were the sheriff and Jeanette an item? He seemed a little more worried than normal for any regular citizen. Nash smiled to himself.

"Yes, but I'm fine, Jack." She waved off his concern. "Nash stepped in before Clay could do anything but slap me."

The sheriff turned to Nash again. "You must be tougher than you look. Usually, it takes a couple men to take Clay down when he's had a few."

Nash shot a surprised glance at Jeanette before meeting Carter's gaze. "You're kidding me, right? I'm a few inches taller than him, and outweigh him by at least fifty pounds, and mine's all muscle. He wasn't that difficult to handle."

Clay huffed and mumbled, "If my brother were here, he'd hand you your ass."

"Maybe, but you aren't your brother, are you, Clay? I'll deal with Robinson when he comes looking for me."

Jeanette's worried expression caught Nash's attention. He smiled at her and leaned over the bar to pat her hand.

"Don't worry, Jeanette. I've had the shit kicked out of me for most of my life. I'm a lot tougher than I look, and, like I said, I'm not afraid of Robinson or anyone else."

Carter rested his hand on Nash's shoulder. "Son, there are men out there you should be careful of, and Robinson is one of them."

Before Nash could ask why, Carter turned back to Clay.

"Let's go, Clay. I have to book you for assault."

"What the hell for? I only slapped her. It wasn't like I beat her or anything like that," Clay protested when Carter lifted him from the chair and cuffed him.

"Drunk and disorderly as well." Carter shot a glance

at Nash. "Actually, I'm charging you with two counts of assault. Rhodes there looks like he might have some injuries."

Most of Nash's wounds were from the incident that had landed him in the hospital, but he wasn't going to argue with the sheriff. He'd spent his life avoiding the police. After Carter had dragged a protesting Clay out, Nash sighed and turned back to the bar, rubbing his hand over his face.

"You look about done in, young man," Jeanette observed, as she took a broom and started cleaning up the mess they'd made.

"I am, and the painkillers don't help. I hate being on this shit. Hate the way it makes me feel." Nash shuddered, shaking off the weight of violence from his shoulders. "So tell me about Robinson? Why are all of you scared of him? Sounds like he's just a small-town bully."

Jeanette leaned the broom against a chair and sat next to Nash. She glared at the bottles lined up along the shelves behind the bar.

"Robinson cooks meth and has his pack sell it to the people around here. Hell, they even go into the bigger towns and cities to sell that poison. He grows weed and sells that as well. He's our local drug dealer. No one wants to cross him because he's crazy and won't hesitate to kill anyone who gets in his way."

Nash wasn't shocked by what Jeanette was saying. Hell, he'd grown up with men like that in Nashville. Some of his closest acquaintances were like Robinson. There was only one member of his club he considered a friend, and Ten was no killer. He wasn't even an enforcer like Nash.

"I have first-hand knowledge of how drugs can mess everyone up, not just the people who take them. Dealers get just as addicted to the high of breaking the law as the addicts do to the drugs." Nash had too many memories racing around his brain to be comfortable with the topic.

"Did you ever sell or do drugs?"

He shook his head. "No, I never did drugs. Hate the idea

of not being in control. Tried weed once and hated it. As for selling them, I never personally did it, but my club did, and I had to protect the product and the money."

Jeanette smiled. "Good. I don't want a junkie working for me. You see how well it went with Clay there. I wouldn't be surprised if he's been sampling his brother's stuff."

Nash stood and stretched carefully. "Is there a motel in town I can get a room at?"

"Oh, I have a trailer out behind the bar you can use. I went in and cleaned it yesterday, so it's all good. The electricity and water are turned on. You won't have to worry about that."

"How much do I owe you for it?"

She wrinkled her nose while she thought. "Hell, I made the last tenant pay two-fifty, but that seems a lot to ask when you're only going to be here for a short time."

Nash thought about the money he had. He'd cleaned out all of his bank accounts when he'd left Nashville and hadn't really spent any of it, except on gas and food. He could afford to pay Jeanette the amount she asked without worrying about it.

"Tell you what? Why don't I work at your bar for room and board? That way you don't have to worry about getting all those pesky papers filled out for the employment people."

"Staying as far under the radar as you can? Are you sure the police aren't after you? Because if they are, once Jack runs your name, they'll know where you are," Jeanette pointed out.

"I was cleared, so the law has no reason to want me. It's all my so-called friends who are looking for me." He chuckled. "Renewing my friendships with them isn't in my best interest."

Jeanette laughed while handing him a set of keys. "Here are the keys to the trailer. Pull your bike around back and lie down for a while. When you get up, if you feel like it, come back over, and I'll show you what you need to do."

Nash bent and brushed a kiss over Jeanette's cheek.

"Thank you, ma'am. I appreciate you being willing to help me out."

She patted his biceps. "Don't worry, dear. We helped each other out, and I think you're going to have more to do than bartend. Robinson isn't going to let this go. He'll want to pay me back for firing Clay."

"I'll be here to keep you and your property safe. I might not be a hundred percent, but I'm still breathing, and I don't back down from a fight until I'm dead."

"That's what I'm afraid of," Jeanette said as Nash walked away from her.

He went outside and climbed on his bike. After riding it around the side of the bar, he saw the doublewide trailer sitting behind the building. Good thing he'd be working nights mostly, because there wouldn't be any way to block out the noise from The Watering Hole.

Nash parked the bike right next to the front porch and entered. It was clean and nice, and didn't have the lingering hint of despair most trailers Nash was familiar with had. This one actually looked like whoever took care of it gave a shit.

Exhaustion kicked in so, after bringing in his bags, he stripped and climbed into bed. The sheets still had their freshly laundered scent, and he relaxed, giving his aching body a vacation from his messed-up life.

Chapter Two

Stepping out onto his back porch, Cullen sniffed the air. He wanted to go for a run, but it wasn't always safe to go out. Even though Cullen was stronger than most men, he couldn't defend himself against those who would try to teach him a lesson. Being a lone wolf in Fallen Creek made life difficult at times, but he had no interest in working for Robinson.

He turned his gaze toward the town as a strange new scent captured his attention. It was definitely different from the normal smells he tasted on the breezes blowing from Fallen Creek, or the foul odors coming from Robinson's land. Cullen tried to avoid that place as much as possible. It took days for his nose to recover from the stench.

Instinct told him that whatever — or whoever — had blown into town would change Fallen Creek — and his life — forever. Yet Cullen didn't want to be changed in any way. He liked his life the way it was, even if it was lonely and tedious. Living on his small ranch and taking care of his horses and cattle made the days bearable most of the time.

There was no one around, so Cullen closed his eyes and allowed his wolf out. The beast flowed over him, taking his human form and morphing it into the creature that shared his soul.

When it was over, a large gray-black wolf stood on the porch. He threw back his head and howled, singing to the moon. He loved running along the plains and among the foothills. The wind in the leaves of the trees spoke of exotic places and marvelous adventures, yet the wolf never had any urge to travel beyond the borders of his land.

Of course, it could be because, in his human form, he had traveled the world over, doing everything and anything to discover himself. The wolf didn't care about all of that. He was interested in simple things — territory, mating and food.

Cullen had gotten two of the three things, and if mating opportunities were few and far between, he couldn't complain. He knew if he ever wanted a mate, he'd have to head to a big city to find a like-minded man, because there wasn't any way he'd find what he wanted in Fallen Creek. Hell, Cullen wanted nothing to do with the gay men in town, since most of them were part of Robinson's pack.

He leaped off the verandah and landed lightly in the grass. He dropped to his side and rolled with exuberance on the dirt. It was wonderful to be free of human worries for a while and experience the natural world at its finest.

After getting back to his feet, Cullen raced for the trees. It had been over a week since he'd run last. Unfortunately, he'd crossed paths with some of Robinson's feeble-minded, muscle-bound enforcers. They'd beaten him up and warned him about what would happen if they caught him out alone again.

He snorted. Like they could scare him. Sure, they would beat him up again, but simply because he was outnumbered. The truth of the matter was that Cullen was far stronger than any of them, even Robinson, the Alpha. If he'd been inclined to challenge Robinson, he would've won, yet Cullen had no interest in being a member, let alone the leader of a pack.

Cullen's father and mother had been lone wolves, living their lives outside of pack authority. They'd spent the majority of his childhood moving from place to place, ahead of the packs. A lot of wolves didn't like being on their own. They worked better living in packs.

He'd never learned how to enjoy the company of others. Cullen had found that being alone was much easier than trusting someone never to leave or hurt him. He had no close friends. Hell, Jeanette at The Watering Hole was the one he talked to the most, and he didn't even consider her a good friend.

He caught the intriguing scent he'd smelled earlier and followed it, not caring that he was wandering off his own land and into Robinson's territory. All he could think about was finding out who smelled so interesting.

The trail led into town and to the trailer behind The Watering Hole. He sniffed around the outside, then went to check out the motorcycle parked by it. Whoever rode the cycle was male, and had a scent like Tennessee whiskey and cotton, like he'd come from the south.

Cullen sat by one end of the trailer, knowing it was the bedroom. He allowed the change to wash over him and soon he stood, naked, by the window. Peering through the glass, he spied the stranger on the bed. He couldn't see much, even with his superior eyesight. All he could really make out was blond hair on a white pillowcase.

Inhaling deeply, he realized he could smell medicine. Was the stranger sick or injured in some way? Was it recent or an old wound? Had he gotten help for it?

Cullen reached up and ran his fingers over the scars on his face. They were an outward symbol of the permanent scars on his soul. Another example of why running without a pack could be dangerous to his health.

The stranger rolled over and faced the window. Cullen took a quick glance at the man's face before changing back into his wolf and running off. He couldn't be caught in town—not in either form. If he were caught as a human, Carter would throw him in jail for indecent exposure. If Robinson caught him as a wolf, he'd end up getting in a fight he didn't want to have. Cullen couldn't risk either, so he needed to get home.

When he reached the edge of town, he glanced toward the bar once before hitting the trail back to his land. He'd come into Fallen Creek tomorrow and see what he could find out about the stranger with the enticing scent. Curiosity killed the cat, his mother always said. Well, it might end up killing the wolf if Cullen didn't get a hold of it.

* * * *

Sunlight burned into Cullen's eyes when he woke up in the early morning. He grunted before rolling onto his side and checking his clock. The alarm was due to go off in five minutes, but he figured, since he was awake, he might as well get up.

He climbed out of bed and stretched. His muscles were slightly sore, but that was normal after a long night run. Cullen padded to the bathroom and turned on the water before he looked in the mirror.

The scars running along his cheeks no longer bothered him. He'd grown used to them and the many other scars he wore from different wolves trying to impose their will on him. The story of his life was written on his skin, yet he wouldn't have it any other way.

Cullen didn't worry about shaving. He was going into town, but there'd never been anyone around he'd wanted to impress. A sudden memory from last night hit him and he remembered the stranger sleeping in the trailer behind The Watering Hole. Grimacing, Cullen shook his head and turned away from the mirror.

He might be intrigued by the man's scent, but he wasn't stupid. Strangers in town meant trouble, and Cullen wasn't interested in trouble. He wanted to live his life on his own terms. Cullen had learned his independence from his parents.

After cleaning up and getting dressed, he headed down the hallway to the kitchen. *Thank God for automatic coffee makers.* The smell of freshly brewed coffee hit his nose and he groaned, anticipating the first cup. He poured it and brought it up to his face, inhaling the rich scent. Nothing he loved more than a strong, dark cup of java.

Cullen got his caffeine fix, then started making breakfast

for himself. He didn't have any ranch hands working for him. His herd wasn't big enough to justify anyone else but himself taking care of them. Plus, he didn't like other people on his land — human or not.

Being a powerful Alpha had its advantages because no one bothered him, or they shouldn't. Unfortunately, Robinson wasn't sane and he didn't fear Cullen, even though Cullen could destroy him without taking a deep breath. He knew there would be a time in the future when he'd have to face Robinson. He would defend his territory and his life.

Breakfast finished, he cleaned the kitchen, then headed out to the barn, where he saddled one of his horses before riding out to the herd. His cattle looked fine — fat and happy with the grass they were eating. Later on in the day, he'd bring out a couple of bales of hay for them to snack on as well.

He'd finished riding his fence line yesterday, so he could take the morning and go into town. Maybe stop by The Watering Hole, talk to Jeanette and get a glimpse of the blond and discover what made him smell so good.

Cullen drove into town, nodding at Sheriff Carter as Carter passed him on the road. He dropped off his list of groceries at the store and the list of supplies at the feed store. He'd pick everything up before he left town. The Watering Hole wasn't open yet, so Cullen strolled over to the Day-Glo Diner and took a seat in one of the booths.

"Do you need a menu, Cullen?"

Glancing up, he shook his head in answer to Marta's question. "I'll have my usual."

"All right. I'll bring you a cup of coffee while it's cooking."

He didn't pay any attention to Marta walking away. A tall blond entering the diner caught his attention. Taking a subtle sniff, Cullen determined that it was the same man from the night before. The man looked around, and Cullen didn't drop his eyes. The blond had to know he was the center of attention.

Hell, everyone was staring at the man. It wasn't often

Fallen Creek got visitors. They were so far off the beaten path, so isolated, Cullen had been shocked when he'd found out the county sheriff's office was in this town.

"Nash, why don't you come sit with me?" Jeanette called from the other side of the diner.

Cullen followed Nash with his gaze, trying to see the man's ass under the leather jacket. He couldn't catch sight of anything, though, and he was surprised by how disappointed he felt by that. Something about Nash called to him and Cullen wasn't happy about it. He didn't want to become fascinated with anyone, especially a guy. At least not here in Fallen Creek.

"Here's your coffee, Cullen." Marta set it in front of him and glanced in the direction of Nash. "He's Jeanette's new bartender. Apparently, Clay showed up last night drunk and belligerent toward her. She fired him and he hit her."

Cullen growled, and Marta shot him a look.

"How bad?"

"Just a slap. I think she might have a small bruise, but that Nash guy stepped in and took Clay down. Carter arrested Clay and tossed him in jail." She rolled her eyes. "Not sure how long he'll be in there after Robinson gets to town."

"Carter's not scared of Robinson, even though he should be. Not just because he's a wolf, but because he's fucking crazy. I've been in this town for a long time and I've seen a lot of people try to stand up to Robinson with no results." Cullen spoke softly.

Marta was a wolf and a member of Robinson's pack, but she knew what her Alpha was like. If she could, she'd have left a while ago, yet she couldn't leave her pups behind. Marta's husband was firmly under Robinson's thumb, and the Alpha would never let the young ones go.

"No one's warned Carter about the wolf part. He's an out-of-towner. You know it's going to come down to you taking care of Robinson, Cullen. I don't know why you don't just do that." She frowned at him.

Cullen shook his head. "I'm not interested in leading a

25

pack, Marta. Plus, I'm hoping someone in your pack will step up and take him down without my help."

Marta didn't say anything, just turned around and walked over to where Nash and Jeanette sat. She poured them coffee and took their orders. Cullen kept his head down while still managing to study Nash. Even though all he could see was the back of Nash's head, Cullen learned some things about the stranger.

Nash had a deep sexy laugh, which Cullen heard over the murmur of the other diner customers. He also had a husky voice with a honey-dipped drawl. Goosebumps rose on Cullen's skin when he heard Nash talk. He curled his upper lip, not liking the sensations.

He didn't want or need to be attracted to the handsome blond. Cullen enjoyed being the outcast of the town. He liked being the wolf no one messed with, not even Robinson for the most part. He was sure feeling desire for Nash would only bring about disaster.

"Here's your food." Marta almost dropped the plate in front of him. "Why don't you go over there and join them? Jeanette wouldn't have a problem, and you could see what the guy looks like from the front."

Cullen shot her an annoyed look, hoping she didn't notice the fear rushing through him. He'd never done anything to make the townspeople think he was gay. It was a lot less hassle to have them believe he was anti-social.

"I'm fine where I'm at," he spoke, snarling slightly.

She backed down, like he knew she would. He might not have a pack, but he was an Alpha, and every non-Alpha wolf submitted to him, whether he led their pack or not. He watched Marta walk away before shaking his head. There was no need to have gotten growly with her. She'd just been making a suggestion, and it was his own fear that had made him think she'd been giving him orders.

He was halfway through his meal when the diner door slammed open. He didn't look up, just wrinkled his nose in disgust when the scent of unwashed man and dirty wolf reached him. Robinson had arrived in town.

"Where's the bitch who put my brother in jail?" the Alpha yelled.

Cullen glanced over at Jeanette, whose face was tight with fear, but who also wasn't hiding. She'd known Robinson would come looking for her, and there'd never been any 'back down' in Jeanette's makeup.

"I'm here, Robinson." Jeanette stood, her hands braced on her table.

Nash stood and moved, taking his place beside the older woman. Well, Cullen had to give it to the man. He might be a stranger, but he wasn't a coward. Even though Cullen hadn't heard the full recounting of what had happened with Clay, anyone who could take the crazy motherfucker down was tough in his own right.

Cullen shoveled his last bite of food in, then wiped his mouth before standing. He kept an eye on what was happening across the diner while he pulled out his wallet and tossed some money next to his plate.

Robinson started to invade Jeanette's personal space, but Nash eased between them, keeping the angry wolf away from her. Cullen strolled closer, and the two scrawny wolves flanking Robinson caught a whiff of his scent. They whirled around to face him, and he almost gagged in disgust.

Shit, they looked terrible, and he knew why. Crystal meth was how Robinson made his living, along with various other illegal drugs. His pack cooked and sold meth everywhere there was a demand and, unfortunately, business had been booming.

It looked like no one had warned them about sampling their product. The two enforcers facing Cullen were obviously addicts. Their teeth were rotting and yellowed. Their skin was sallow and breaking out. Their hands shook with the need driving them.

It wouldn't be hard to take them down if they made a move. Cullen propped his hands on his hips and glared at them. It was a good thing Robinson wasn't paying any attention to them—he would have killed them both if he saw how they lowered their gazes and tilted their heads, offering their necks to Cullen.

"No one throws my brother in jail, bitch. I told you that when you threatened to do it the last time." Robinson's spittle landed on Nash's leather coat.

Nash's disgusted grimace made Cullen want to laugh, but he kept his face expressionless. Any sound would give his position away, and he wanted to see what Nash was going to do about Robinson.

"You need to back the fuck up," Nash ordered. "And you need to watch your mouth. No one talks to a lady like that in my presence."

Robinson snorted. "A lady? All I see is an old—"

Before he could get the next word out, Nash had his hand wrapped around Robinson's throat, then he lifted him off the ground. A pretty impressive feat considering Robinson was almost as tall as Nash and probably weighed fifty pounds more.

"I told you to speak respectfully to her." Nash shook Robinson hard.

The Alpha struggled and waved his hands, trying to get his two guards' attention, but they were focused entirely on Cullen.

"You really should put him down," Cullen suggested from where he stood.

Nash shot him a glance. "Or what? You'll come after me?"

Cullen chuckled. "Hell, no. I don't really care what the fuck you do with him. I'm just worried the rest of his gang will come in here, and I don't want them to destroy the diner."

Nash narrowed his pretty blue eyes and studied Cullen. Jeanette put her hand on his arm.

"Don't worry, Nash. Cullen's a good man. He isn't here to help Robinson one bit."

After giving Robinson another hard shake, Nash tossed him into the other two men. They fought for their balance and Cullen shook his head. Robinson and his pack gave all wolves a bad name. He kept his hands on his hips, not offering to help Robinson at all.

The Alpha whirled and snarled at Cullen, who raised his eyebrows in surprise. Robinson had never offered any sort of challenge toward Cullen, since his wolf knew that Cullen's wolf was far stronger. Yet Cullen also understood that Robinson wasn't really thinking clearly.

Robinson and his Betas paled and paused for a moment before turning on Nash. Cullen decided not to step in unless it looked like Nash was in trouble. So far, it appeared the human could handle himself.

"Who the fuck are you? Don't ever touch me again," Robinson ordered Nash.

The blond snorted. "I'm Jeanette's new bartender, and as long as you don't threaten her again, I won't touch you. God knows I don't want to catch anything from you."

"Jeanette, you know better than to fire Clay. I told you what I'd do if you did."

Jeanette shrugged. "I'm not afraid of you and your punks, Robinson. Clay is a drunk and an addict. I'm not paying him to go on binges and not work. I'm not taking him back either, so if you bail him out, don't bring him back to me."

Robinson took a step toward Jeanette, and Cullen had had enough. He growled low in his throat, causing Robinson and his Betas to freeze. Strolling around them, he ignored the weird glances Nash shot him. He stepped right up into Robinson's personal space.

"I suggest you leave right now, Robinson. Go and harass Carter to see if he'll let Clay out, but I doubt it, since this isn't the first time he's done shit like this."

Cullen curled his lip up, baring his teeth. It was a silent challenge to Robinson, but Cullen wasn't worried about any response. The Alpha wasn't interested in getting his ass whipped yet.

"Just remember, O'Murphy, you're going to do that one too many times," Robinson warned.

"And what will happen then? You're going to do something to me?" Cullen chuckled. "I'm not particularly scared, Robinson. Now get out of here."

He took one step toward the three wolves and their courage broke. He laughed as they tripped over each other in their rush to race out of the diner.

"Thanks for stepping in, Cullen," Marta said from where she stood behind the counter.

"No problem. I wasn't going to let them start anything in here." He turned to look at Jeanette. Without thinking, he reached out and placed his knuckle under her chin, lifting it enough for him to see the bruise on her cheek. "Clay do that to you?"

Jeanette dropped her gaze and tilted her head to the side slightly. The submissive gesture eased his aggressive urges for the moment. Cullen tamped down his need to chase after Robinson and tear out his throat, then hunt down Clay and do the same to him.

"Yes. He was drunk and didn't like the idea of me firing him. So he took it out on me. Of course, Nash was here and stopped it from being worse." Jeanette gestured to the man standing next to her.

Cullen hadn't forgotten Nash. All his instincts — wolf and human — knew exactly where Nash was and wanted him to grab the man and bury his nose at the base of Nash's neck. That wouldn't do, since he wasn't going to out himself in front of the entire town, and he wasn't going to risk getting punched for his trouble.

He glanced over at Nash, who stood with his arms folded over his chest. Nash studied Cullen without showing an ounce of submission and, for some reason, that hit Cullen's buttons. He might be an Alpha, but he didn't want any of his lovers being too submissive.

"Thank you for protecting Jeanette, though you've managed to gain yourself an enemy. Well, actually, you've gained the hatred of an entire pack of crazy jackasses."

"Cowboy, the day idiots like those three scare me is the

day I'll hang my leathers up and hit the rocking chair."

Cullen wasn't sure what to say. He'd never had anyone talk to him like that. He was used to being respected, though he'd never really figured out why. Obviously, his scars didn't bother Nash. From the man's attitude, Cullen had the feeling it took a lot to intimidate him.

"Cullen O'Murphy, meet Nash Rhodes, my new bartender. He's living in the trailer behind the bar." Jeanette introduced them.

"Nice to meet you." Cullen didn't offer to shake hands. He didn't like the way his body was reacting to Nash's closeness.

Nash didn't seem offended by Cullen's lack of manners. The blond nodded and turned to smile at Jeanette. "I have to head back to my trailer. Got to set up an appointment with a doctor, or else my mother will be coming to hunt me down."

Jeanette smiled. "Go on, Nash. Meet me at the bar around two, and I'll show you what you need to do. Not that you haven't worked a bar before or anything, but there are a few things I do a little differently."

"Everyone has their own way of doing things. I'm a quick learner." Nash nodded at Cullen before strolling away.

Cullen couldn't help but watch the man walk out of the diner. It wasn't until Jeanette bumped his shoulder that he realized he'd been staring. He glanced down at the older lady, and she winked.

"He is rather pretty, isn't he?" she whispered under her breath.

Cullen shot a look around, making sure they were alone. "I don't know what you're talking about."

"Of course you don't. I was just making a comment. The girls are going to love him." Jeanette's expression was pure innocence.

He wasn't going to chase after that line of conversation. Jeanette was a smart woman. She could have noticed some signals he hadn't even known he was sending. Hopefully, no one else had noticed it, because he didn't want to have to look over his shoulder for that reason.

Chapter Three

Nash stared at the wall behind the bar, but he wasn't studying the bottles of liquor or even looking at his reflection in the mirror. He was remembering Cullen O'Murphy, the big cowboy he'd met at the diner.

The man was huge, far bigger than most of the bikers Nash had come across. Yet Cullen wasn't fat. He had the feeling that every inch of the cowboy was pure hard muscle. Nash shifted a little, wishing he didn't like how Cullen looked so much. It would make his life easier if he didn't have to fight an attraction to the man, especially in a small town like Fallen Creek.

He'd managed to scratch his itch in Nashville without any of his fellow club members finding out, but since the population of Fallen Creek had to be beyond small, he doubted there would be any way he could hide getting involved with Cullen.

Grunting, Nash shook his head and turned away. He had to clean the glasses and get ready for the evening crowd. No point in thinking about Cullen. There wasn't any way that cowboy was gay, no matter how much Nash might wish him to be.

"I forgot to thank you for stepping in with Robinson for me at the diner."

Looking up, he found Jeanette standing on the other side of the bar and he smiled. "No problem, ma'am. Wasn't about to let him beat on you any more than I let his brother."

"Still, I appreciate it, especially when it wasn't your fight to begin with. The trouble between Robinson and me goes way back." Jeanette slid onto one of the stools and propped her elbows on the bar.

He paused in the middle of drying a glass and looked at her. "Would that O'Murphy guy have stepped in if I wasn't there? He didn't look scared of Robinson, but he also didn't look like he wanted to get involved."

Jeanette snorted. "Cullen would've stepped in, and Robinson would've backed down even quicker than he did. Robinson doesn't want to mess with Cullen, and as long as Robinson leaves him alone, Cullen won't interfere with Robinson's activities."

"Really?"

"Well, for the most part Cullen stays out of what goes on around town. He likes to be left alone, yet I know if I need him, he'll help me out." Jeanette shook her head. "I wish he'd just get fed up with Robinson and beat the shit out of the jackass. It would make all of our lives easier."

Nash gave up trying not to look interested in Cullen and the dynamics of the entire town. He might have only arrived last night, but he could tell there were undercurrents in Fallen Creek that could swell into a raging river if the right catalyst showed up.

He braced his hands on the edge of the bar and met Jeanette's gaze. "Why hasn't he done something about Robinson?"

Jeanette shrugged, tracing a circle on the counter. "Not completely sure. Maybe he doesn't want the responsibility that comes with taking Robinson out. Cullen's a lone wolf. He likes living on his ranch without visitors or hands to help him. He comes to town once or twice a month but doesn't stay very long. I was surprised to see him this morning. He'd been in for supplies last week."

"He could've gotten tired of his own cooking," Nash suggested.

"He never has before. I wonder if something happened to make him come in." Jeanette pursed her lips while she seemed to be thinking.

Nash still didn't understand why Cullen wouldn't do

something about Robinson if he could. "It was obvious Robinson and his goons were afraid of O'Murphy, so why doesn't the cowboy use that fear and get Robinson out of here?"

The bar owner sighed and her troubled gaze met Nash's. "There's more going on here than you know, Nash, and I don't think you want to know the dirty secrets Fallen Creek holds. It's probably best you don't ask any more questions."

"Or what? I'll get in trouble with the sheriff or Robinson? Neither one of them scares me."

And it was true. There was only one person in the world who scared Nash, and he'd left the man behind when he'd driven away from Nashville. He hoped Union never figured out where he'd gone because he didn't want to deal with the president of his club. The man was psychotic and blamed Nash for all the shit that had gone down, which had ended with Nash in the hospital.

"You don't know Robinson, Nash. He's insane and totally unafraid of anyone, except Cullen. He's run this town for so long, he doesn't believe anyone can touch him."

Nash went back to setting the glasses out for the night. "Thanks for the warning, ma'am, but I'm not going to run away from a fight. If Robinson brings trouble to you or me, I'll stand and face him."

"I was afraid you'd say that. Hopefully, Robinson will stay away from you and not push the issue. You don't plan on being here very long, and I don't want anything more to happen to you." Jeanette stood. "Have you talked to your mother lately?"

Nash blinked, unnerved by the quick change in subject. "Umm...not yet. I'm not looking forward to telling her I had to stop for a while to rest. She wasn't happy about me driving out to see her in the first place."

"Of course she wasn't. I'm sure your mother doesn't want her little boy to hurt, and riding that motorcycle isn't conducive to you healing faster." Jeanette leaned over the bar and patted his hand. "Go call her. She's probably worried sick about you."

She was right. He'd had, like, twenty messages on his phone from her in the last several hours. The only reason he hadn't called her back was because he didn't want to listen to her yell at him for riding instead of flying. She didn't understand why he wasn't willing to leave his bike behind. Ten would have taken care of it for him, but he didn't want to risk Union getting hold of it and destroying it.

His Harley was the only possession he cared about. None of the other stuff he'd abandoned in Nashville mattered to him. Nash had never kept anything personal in his apartment. All that stuff was stored somewhere no one knew about. Maybe if he found a place to settle after visiting his mom, he'd send Ten the key and have him box it all up for him.

Nash went outside and sat on the steps of his trailer. He pulled out his phone and stared at it for a moment. While he was working up the courage to dial his mother's number, the phone rang.

He answered it. "Hey, Ten."

"Where the hell are you, man?" Ten's voice ripped from the phone, fear and anger warring in his tone.

"I had to get out of there, bro. I couldn't let Union find me. You know what he'd have done." Nash pressed his hand to his side and grimaced.

One of Clay's punches had landed right on Nash's ribs and, while they were no longer broken, they weren't completely healed either. Nash had popped some more painkillers this morning to deal with the ache.

"I know, but you could've told me you were leaving," Ten complained.

Nash shook his head, even though his friend couldn't see him. "No, I couldn't have. Union would beat the shit out of you if he thought you had any idea where I went. I'm not telling you anything, Ten. I don't want you hurt. Just know I'm okay, and when I get settled somewhere, I'll call you."

Ten sighed. "Dude, I can't believe you bolted like that. I

thought we were friends."

"We are. Hell, man, you're my best friend, but I couldn't stay in Nashville one more day. I'd already been there for too long after I got out of the hospital. There are things I can't tell you yet, and things you're better off not knowing about me." Nash swallowed around the lump in his throat.

He'd never mentioned being gay to Ten. While he didn't think his friend would be upset about his sexual preference, it had just been easier to hide that part of him from everyone in the club. It would have given Union one more reason to hunt his ass down and put him in the ground.

Ten grunted. "I get it, Nash. It just hurt, you know. You leaving like that? But you're doing okay, right? You're not pushing too hard?"

"I was, but decided to make a stop and rest for a week or two before I head out again. Found a little out-of-the-way place to crash and get more of my energy back." He chuckled. "I was fucking crazy to take off like that. Two hours out of Nashville, I knew I was stupid, but I'd been planning on leaving for a while."

He bit his tongue. Why had he admitted that, even to Ten? Nash had kept his plans so close to his vest for so long, and he'd never thought he'd spill the beans like that.

"Really? How long have you been thinking about leaving, Nash? And why didn't you say a word to me about being unhappy?"

Nash pulled the phone away from his ear and stared at it for a moment. When had his best friend turned into a girl who wanted to know Nash's feelings? He gave himself a mental slap. That wasn't nice or fair. Ten had always been more in touch with his emotions than Nash had, and it didn't make him a girly man either.

He put the phone back to his ear and said, "Because you're Union's nephew, Ten, and I didn't want him to know I was thinking about leaving before I was ready to do it. You know he'd have done whatever he had to do to keep me in the club."

"You've been a good enforcer for him, and he doesn't want to have to train a new one." Ten hesitated for a moment before continuing, "Of course, he also doesn't want you going off where he can't control you. You know too much about the inner workings of the club."

And that was the entire crux of the situation. There were things Nash knew that not even Ten was privy to, and it could mean his life if Union caught up with him. Yet Nash wasn't just running from Union and the club. He was running from the police and what they wanted from him. He was also trying to outpace his memories and the knowledge of all the harm he'd done for most of his life.

"That's why I won't tell you where I am, Ten. We both know Union won't shy away from torturing you to find out my whereabouts. It won't matter that you're his nephew, which is why you need to stay away from him. Don't let him get a hold of you," Nash reminded his best friend.

"I know." Ten sighed. "All right. I'd better let you go. The guys are coming over and we're going for a ride. Call me when you've found someplace safe. I won't ask where it is or anything like that."

"Take care, Ten. I do miss you, bro."

They hung up, and Nash let his hands dangle between his knees while he banged his head against the side of his trailer. *Christ!* He was an idiot. He should have known Ten would take his leaving hard. They'd been inseparable since they were sixteen, when Nash had gotten involved with the club. Ten had a hard time making friends — mostly because he was extremely shy, but having an uncle who was the head of the local motorcycle club didn't help either.

"You might hurt something else if you keep that up."

Nash jumped to his feet when he heard the voice come from beside him. He whirled to find Cullen standing there, hands stuffed into his back pockets and a frown on his face.

He tried not to focus on the way Cullen's faded jeans pulled tight over his groin and gave a hint of a tantalizing bulge there. *Nothing there for you, Nash.* Disappointment surged through him for a second.

Would he ever be able to show attraction toward a man without worrying about getting his ass kicked? Maybe when he got out to Santa Monica and his mother's house, he'd be able to go up to San Fran and hang out in the Castro. He'd heard it was a good place for a guy like him. He'd be able to find others who liked what he liked and not have to be as worried about being beaten to a pulp.

Cullen cleared his throat and Nash blinked. His face heated when he realized he'd been staring at Cullen.

"What do you want?"

Cullen shrugged. "Hell if I know. I was on my way to my truck. It's time to get out of this fucking town and back to my ranch. Somehow, I found my way over here and saw you hitting your head on your trailer."

"Don't worry. My mom always said my head was the hardest part of my body," Nash joked.

"Hmmm...too bad," Cullen murmured. His gaze trailed from Nash's head, then lingered for a moment on his crotch, before finishing at his feet.

Nash tilted his head, sure he hadn't heard Cullen right. There was no way the man was gay. It was just wishful thinking on Nash's part. Cullen cleared his throat again, shifting his weight from one foot to the other. Cullen's full upper lip curled, baring his teeth, and Nash got the feeling the cowboy wasn't happy about being nervous.

Why was the man nervous? It wasn't like Nash was going to do anything to him, even though Nash would have liked to drag Cullen into the trailer, tie him to the bed and lick every inch of him.

"I just wanted to warn you about Robinson and his pack again. They aren't people to mess with."

Nash started to say something, but Cullen held up his hand.

"I don't doubt you can take care of yourself. You look like a tough guy, but Robinson and his pack aren't sane. They don't care about being fair." Cullen shook his head.

Snorting, Nash sat back down on the steps. "Don't worry. I'm used to dealing with crazy people. I don't expect anyone to fight fair. I didn't learn how to be nice when it comes to fighting."

"Good, because Robinson will be coming after you at some point or another. You made him look weak in front of his men and the townspeople. He won't let that stand. Keep an eye out. He won't announce the attack. More than likely, he'll send some of his pack to come and teach you a lesson." Cullen eased over to prop his hip against the rail next to Nash.

"Why do you call his gang a pack?"

Cullen stared at the back of The Watering Hole. "They remind me of a pack of rabid dogs, going after the weak or the people who don't have anyone to fight for them."

"If you feel that way, why don't you do something about it? Looked to me like Robinson and his men were scared of you." Nash eyed Cullen. "All it takes is one guy to stand up to him, and the rest of the folks will gather behind."

"Robinson has always been afraid of me, but, trust me, it doesn't matter to these people." Cullen waved in a vague circle, apparently encompassing the town. "They're so frightened of the asshole, they won't do anything about him."

Nash grimaced. "I'm not sure it's any of my business. I'm not going to be around for long. Got places to be."

"And people to run from," Cullen suggested.

Nash didn't get upset at Cullen's comment. Whether the man was guessing or had figured it out, Nash didn't care. It was true. He was running as far away from Union and the gang as he could get.

He wanted to live and he'd accepted the truth that if he had stayed in Nashville, he would've been dead two days after he'd gotten out of the hospital. Maybe it was the coward's way of dealing with things, but Nash didn't care if Cullen thought he was yellow. He was alive and Union had no idea where he was. That was the important thing.

"Aren't we all running from something or someone?" He leaned back on his elbows and looked up at Cullen.

Cullen dropped his gaze to meet Nash's and nodded. "That's the truth."

"Who are you running from?"

Nash wasn't sure why he asked the question. He didn't want to know anything about Cullen. Nash wasn't looking to make friends in Fallen Creek, even though he could probably count Jeanette as one now. Yet Nash's libido had taken over, and while it would have rather pressed his mouth against Cullen's, it had decided that learning more about the man might be safer.

"I'm not running from anyone," Cullen said.

Nash started to disagree when he saw sadness fill Cullen's eyes.

"I'm running away from memories. That's why I live so far out of town and have made no effort to make friends. Having people around who care for you can cause problems I don't want to deal with." Cullen scrubbed his hand over his head.

"I get it."

Without thinking, Nash reached out and laid his hand on Cullen's hip where it rested against the railing. Cullen stiffened, and Nash realized what he'd done. He yanked his hand away and shot to his feet.

"You probably have things to do. Thanks for the warning, and I'll take your advice and keep my eyes out for Robinson."

Cullen growled low in his throat and, before Nash could move any farther away, Cullen grabbed his arms and jerked him close.

Their lips met in a hard kiss. The shock of Cullen's sudden movement caused Nash to gasp, and Cullen took advantage. He slipped his tongue in and teased Nash's.

Nash usually took the lead in any encounter he had. Maybe it was because he picked up guys who were smaller than him. Maybe it was because he was part of a motorcycle gang and his lovers assumed he wouldn't submit to them.

Yet, deep inside, Nash didn't like being in charge. He'd always wanted his lovers to tell him what to do and make him submit to their control. Something told him Cullen wasn't going to roll over and let Nash fuck him, which was fine with Nash.

He reached up and buried his fingers in Cullen's thick salt-and-pepper hair. He held on but didn't demand anything. Nash participated in the kiss, rubbing his lips over Cullen's and pressing his body against the hard form of the man in front of him.

Christ! Cullen had muscles on top of muscles. Being a cowboy and wrangling cattle must be good for making hot men out of boys. Of course, Cullen was older than Nash, but it didn't look like age was slowing him down.

Nash groaned when Cullen grabbed his ass and dragged him even closer. They ground their groins together, and Nash grunted. He broke the kiss to pant. When he got some breath, he tugged Cullen toward the trailer.

"Let's take this inside," he suggested.

A door slammed and Cullen stiffened. Nash hated to admit he wasn't surprised that Cullen stepped away. He didn't say a word as the man spun around and stalked off around the side of the bar.

Sighing, Nash went into his trailer. He grabbed a beer out of the fridge and sat at the rickety table. After taking a sip, he pressed his hand to his ribs. A dull ache resided there, reminding Nash of all the reasons why he needed to stay away from Cullen and not get involved with anyone in Fallen Creek.

Aside from his mom and Ten, there'd been only one other person he'd cared for, and that person had turned out to be the reason why he'd ended up in the hospital and under the close scrutiny of the police.

Nash rested his forehead on the surface of the table. He wasn't only running away from Union, he was running from the memory of a pretty smile and bright blue eyes.

Shit! He had been such an idiot, and if Ten had known, he would've beaten some sense into him. Unfortunately, Nash had thought he could handle everything, not thinking with his head, but with his heart and his dick.

A knock on his door brought his head up and he stood to see who was there. Jeanette was on the other side, a smile on her face.

"I wanted to know if you were coming to work. I'm getting ready to open."

"Oh, sorry. Guess I lost track of time." He dumped out the rest of his beer and set the bottle in the sink.

He walked over to the back door of the bar with Jeanette. They didn't talk until after they'd gotten the chairs off the tables and the doors unlocked. Finally, Jeanette propped her elbows on the bar and eyed Nash.

"Was that Cullen I saw pulling out of the parking lot a little while ago?"

Nash shrugged. "I have no idea. What makes you think I'd know? The guy seemed like an asshole."

"That's true. Cullen is very rough around the edges. If I didn't know better, I'd think he'd been raised by wolves."

There was something in the tone of Jeanette's voice that made Nash glance at her.

"Are his parents still around?"

He gritted his teeth after the question slipped out of his mouth. Damn, he hadn't wanted to know anything else about Cullen. It was bad enough he would go to bed remembering how Cullen's lips had felt on his, and how the man smelled like nothing Nash had ever smelled before.

Jeanette shook her head. "I don't know, but I've never met them. He doesn't talk about his family. Of course, he doesn't talk about anything all that much. It was only after several months that I found out he wasn't mute."

"There's not much conversation to be had with cattle," Nash pointed out.

She chuckled. "True, but he could come into town whenever he wanted to talk to someone. I just don't think he likes people all that much, and I know he hates Robinson with a consuming passion."

Nash stopped wiping down the bar and met Jeanette's gaze. "Why doesn't he do something about that, then? Why does he allow Robinson to continue to terrorize this town when he could do something about it?"

Jeanette breathed deeply and shook her head. "Cullen doesn't want to get involved in other people's problems. Also, there are other issues this town is dealing with, Nash, and just one person can't fix it all."

Nash grunted. He was pretty sure there was only one problem and its name was Robinson. Once they'd cut the head off the snake, the rest of Robinson's gang would slip away — Nash doubted there was anyone strong enough to take over for him.

"I can tell you that what's wrong with this town goes far deeper than Robinson and his pack. It would take more than Cullen to clean up all the shit going on." Jeanette looked like she was about to say something more, but the door opened and Sheriff Carter walked in.

Nash could tell the sheriff had gotten Nash's file from the Nashville police department, and the man wasn't happy.

"Sheriff Carter, what can we do for you?" Jeanette gestured for the sheriff to sit on the stool next to her.

"I need to talk to Rhodes alone, Jeanette."

She didn't ask why, just nodded toward the office door. "You can use my office. I'll call you if I need your help. It's still early, though I expect there'll be a crowd. Everyone's going to come and check out the new guy."

Nash followed the sheriff to the office, not looking forward to the upcoming conversation.

Chapter Four

"What the fuck were you thinking?" Cullen muttered as he stepped from his truck. He slammed the door shut and growled.

What had possessed him to grab Nash and kiss the man like that? Of course, Cullen didn't have to worry about getting his ass beaten by Nash. As tough and in shape as Nash was, there wasn't any way he could take on a full-grown wolf without ending up injured.

Even though he didn't have to worry, why the hell had he decided kissing the damn man was wise? It wasn't like they were hidden from anyone. Hell, Jeanette could have walked out of the bar and seen them in front of Nash's trailer. Anyone wandering around the neighborhood could have seen them and Cullen's secret would have been out.

Cullen had never been ashamed of being gay, but he'd discovered his life was a lot easier if no one knew. Most packs would have used the knowledge to hunt him down and kill him. He'd heard there were packs out there that accepted members who were different, whether because of their sexual preference or because they had physical or mental challenges, but he'd never come across any.

Robinson's pack wasn't one of them. He preferred to have members who didn't think for themselves, but were able-bodied enough to haul his shit to all the distributors. He hated anyone who was different in any way from him.

Cullen snorted. Different meant smarter as well, so Nash was on Robinson's hit list now. He sighed. He was going to get far more entangled in what happened with Nash than he had in any other person's life, and he wasn't happy about that.

Any other person except for one.

He shook his head and grunted. All he wanted was to forget Sara and what had happened to her, but no matter how far he ran and how much he tried to block it out of his mind, the memories crept back in.

Cullen sniffed the air, making sure no one was waiting for him before entering the barn. All he wanted to do was run, but he couldn't shift around his buildings during the day.

He saddled up his favorite mount, a Tobiano Paint gelding. After they were ready, he rode off toward one of his back pastures. He never kept his herd out there, though there was good grass and lots of water. It was too close to Robinson's territory and Cullen didn't trust the bastard not to kill every single head of cattle. He was pretty sure Robinson wouldn't step foot on Cullen's land because the asshole knew Cullen would take on the entire pack to defend his own territory.

It probably didn't make sense to many people that Cullen wouldn't challenge Robinson over what the man was doing to the town and the people living there, but if the Alpha chose to invade Cullen's territory and ranch, Cullen would take his head and mount it on a spike. Too many times Cullen had watched his parents be run off. His father had never stood up for himself, even when he was stronger than the wolves that had hunted them. Cullen had made a vow to himself that he would never give an inch of his own land. Maybe he was a lone wolf without a pack to back him, but he didn't need one.

Cullen shook his head. The only time he wished he'd had friends to help him out was with Sara. If he had, maybe Sara wouldn't have been killed, murdered by an addiction she didn't want to fight, while Cullen had been helpless to do anything.

All Sara's family had told him it wasn't his fault. He'd done all he could, but Sara had loved the meth more than she'd loved him or the rest of her pack. Cullen had tried to get her to rehab, yet she had never admitted to having a problem. Sara had thought she could quit any time she wanted and had kept going back to get more.

Wolves were very susceptible to illicit drugs, especially meth. It was the drug that hit them the hardest and was the most difficult for them to kick. Cullen should be furious about what Robinson was doing to his own pack and the humans around Fallen Creek, but he couldn't bring himself to care.

He'd fought for so long to save his best friend, and watching Sara slide into addiction and waste away from the drugs had destroyed every bit of caring Cullen had in him. Where it probably would've driven most men to seek revenge on the people who'd sold the drugs Sara had been hooked on, all her loss had done was drive him further away from any interaction with humans or wolves. Humans had never meant that much to Cullen anyway. It wasn't that he'd never had much to do with them, he had just never stepped in to keep them from their own destruction.

Nash's image popped into his mind and Cullen snarled under his breath. His gelding huffed softly, reminding him to keep his wolf under control while he rode the horse. Cullen patted the gelding's neck in a quiet apology.

The animals on his ranch had accepted his wolf and weren't afraid of him in either form. He appreciated how smart they were after he'd explained the situation.

Once he arrived at the clearing next to a small stream, he dismounted and removed the gelding's tack. He slipped a halter on before tying the horse to a tree. He made sure the rope was long enough for the gelding to be able to get a drink of water or graze quite a distance from the tree.

Cullen stripped off his clothes and left them with his tack. He allowed his wolf to take over and the shift swept over him. When he could see again, he stood on four paws and shook his entire body. He threw back his head and howled, letting all the wolves in the area know he was around.

Silence reigned in the woods. The other animals, not just

the wolves, knew a top predator was out and they would go to ground, waiting him out. Cullen didn't care – he wasn't interested in hunting anyway.

He ran for an hour or two, exhausting himself to try to get rid of the memory of Nash's hard body against his. The way the man had surrendered to his touch had been amazing, even though Cullen doubted Nash had ever let another man control him like that. Nonetheless, Cullen had the feeling that the human would enjoy submitting and Cullen wanted to be the one who took him.

When he got back to the clearing, he returned to his human form and curled his lip in disgust. As much as he fought it, he knew it would only be a matter of time before he headed back into town and found Nash. He'd be dragging the man back to his ranch for some heavy-duty fucking.

It had been a long time since Cullen had been this attracted to someone. So attracted that he was willing to let go of his normal caution and risk exposing himself to the townspeople. Not that he'd expose himself so much that they would realize he was bisexual, but showing how much he liked Nash was giving away a weakness.

Cullen had learned the hard way never to appear weak in front of people who might be enemies. He gave an annoyed snort. Everyone he met was a potential enemy. Cullen wasn't the type of guy who made friends easily. He was more the one they all tried to avoid. He didn't mind being that person.

It made life simpler when he didn't have to worry about people stopping by his house to chat or asking him for help. He wasn't very helpful either. He had to really care about others to be willing to do anything for them.

He pulled on his clothes then saddled the gelding. It was time to go and check on his herd. Dusk had snuck up on the land, and Cullen rode leisurely over to the other pasture. Inside, his wolf surveyed its territory, pleased with its place in the world. For all that it snarled and growled to put Robinson down whenever Cullen met up with the Alpha,

Cullen's own wolf was a rather laid-back animal.

After making sure his cattle were fine, Cullen went back to the main buildings. He took care of his horse before heading inside. He wandered down the hallway to the kitchen at the back of his house. As he opened the refrigerator door, he had the feeling he wasn't going to find anything he wanted in it. Not even the beer would be what he liked, even though he'd bought it the last time he'd been into town.

The fridge shuddered when he slammed the door shut. *God damn!* He hated this urge shoving him back to Nash. Following that path meant nothing but heartache at the end of the road.

A sudden thought hit him. Nash wasn't going to stick around. He'd be in Fallen Creek for two weeks at the most. Maybe he was the best guy for Cullen to have a fling with. He wouldn't expect more than just some fun, getting off together and releasing some pent-up energy.

Nash didn't strike Cullen as being a sentimental type who believed in love and all that shit. He knew the score and Cullen wouldn't have to worry about breaking his heart.

With those delusional rationalizations firmly in his head, Cullen went to take a shower. He would go back to town and see if he couldn't interest Nash in picking up where they'd left off earlier. Somehow, Cullen doubted the man would say no.

* * * *

After pulling up in front of The Watering Hole an hour later, Cullen turned his truck off and stared at the building. Now that he was here, his decision didn't seem like a good one all of a sudden. There were too many people at the bar. Anyone could see him there, figure out what — and who — he wanted and cause trouble.

He scrubbed his hand over his face, contemplating starting the truck and going back to the ranch. A knock on his window startled him. Cullen glanced over to see Carter standing there.

What did the sheriff want? Cullen didn't roll down the window. He stepped out of the truck—he couldn't very well leave now that someone had seen him.

"Sheriff," he said gruffly, while settling his hat on his head.

"O'Murphy." The sheriff was as cautious around him as every other person in Fallen Creek.

"What's got you out in Jeanette's parking lot? The uniform says you're still on duty." Cullen nodded toward the star on Carter's chest.

Carter turned to study the entrance to the bar. His gaze narrowed slightly, and Cullen's wolf stood at attention. Every instinct—wolf and human—inside Cullen screamed that something was wrong. He took a deep breath, filling his lungs with the warm night air.

A low growl surged from his chest. The sick scent of decay and rot assaulted his nose. Robinson and his pack were approaching and Cullen had a feeling they weren't interested in a night of simply drinking.

"Fuck!"

He didn't acknowledge the sheriff, just took off toward the bar. Cullen had to warn everyone in there. He didn't want anyone else getting hurt, even though he knew Robinson would focus on Jeanette and Nash. Collateral damage would mean hurt humans and destroyed property.

"I've got backup coming," Carter informed him, matching Cullen stride for stride. "I've been sitting out here for most of the night. I figured Robinson wouldn't let the insults go."

"The man's a complete psycho, and he rules his pack with fear. He can't let it look like anyone, especially a stranger, got the better of him. Robinson has to reinforce his power or someone might get the idea he's weak and take his position from him."

"Like you?"

Cullen stopped and turned to look at Carter. "I don't know what you're talking about. Why would I want to take over Robinson's drug business?"

"I didn't mean his illegal activities. I meant take his position as Alpha in the pack."

Shock raced through Cullen at the realization that Carter knew about wolves and shifters. How long had he known and why hadn't he said anything? Before Cullen could ask the questions, Carter shook his head.

"Trust me, O'Murphy, now is not the time to be asking me anything." Carter gestured toward the building. "Go and get everyone out of there. I'll try to delay Robinson."

His surprise didn't wear off until he opened the door of The Watering Hole. He started to turn back. Carter was only human—he wasn't nearly strong enough to keep Robinson from storming into Jeanette's place. The sheriff stared at him and he saw the determination in Carter's gaze. The man would do whatever he had to do to keep the people under his protection from getting hurt. Cullen wouldn't take that away from him.

After turning back to search around the room, Cullen spotted both Jeanette and Nash by the bar. He stepped into the building and silence fell over the crowd. He didn't know why. It could have been shock at seeing him in town twice in one day, but somehow he didn't think that was it.

"Everyone needs to clear out right now," he said, raising his voice slightly, making sure to put all the power of his wolf behind the words.

While humans weren't the same as wolves, they still reacted to authority and dominance. The more submissive ones were already heading toward the door where he stood. Cullen shook his head.

"You need to leave by the back door."

Robinson wouldn't have sent any of his pack to watch the other exits. He didn't have the mental capabilities to multitask like that. The Alpha was more a 'hit them head on' type of fighter, which made Cullen's job easier.

"Is Robinson on his way here?" Jeanette approached him cautiously.

Rage was surging through Cullen at the thought of Robinson hurting Nash, and it was stupid. Nash could take care of himself. He definitely didn't need Cullen's help, yet just the thought of Robinson touching a hair on Nash's head made Cullen's wolf snarl and howl inside.

His eyes must have been glowing, judging by the fearful, wide-eyed gaze Jeanette gave him.

"Yes." He growled. "Carter's stalling him, and backup is on the way, but it won't get here before Robinson gets in."

"You left Carter out there by himself?" Jeanette sounded angry.

Cullen nodded, watching as Nash ushered the humans out of the bar. "It's his job, Jeanette, and he knows what Robinson and the rest of the pack are."

She looked as surprised as Cullen had felt. "Really? Why didn't he say anything?"

"My thoughts exactly but, at the moment, it's not important. You and Nash need to get out of here. If Robinson can't get his hands on you, he might restrict his anger to the furniture instead of people."

Jeanette shook her head. "I'm not letting that rabid dog run me off my own land. He might be the Alpha of this territory, but I rule in my own home and I dare him to try anything with me."

Something flashed in her eyes and Cullen wondered what he'd missed all these years. Jeanette's scent changed into something he'd never smelled before. Who — or what — was Jeanette?

"If you won't leave, then Nash won't either. You and I might be able to survive an attack by Robinson and the pack, but Nash is human and he's already injured. Do you really want him hurt worse because he thinks he has to protect you?"

Jeanette curled her upper lip at him in disgust. "That's a real low blow, Cullen."

"But it worked, didn't it?"

"Yes." She huffed, crossing her arms over her chest. "I

was looking forward to finally handing Robinson's ass to him."

A snort of laughter burst from Cullen. He patted her shoulder and smiled. "I promise to leave Robinson's ass intact so you can take it apart later."

Nash joined them, carrying a good-sized length of lead pipe. "Why did we make everyone leave?"

"I think you know, and you need to take Jeanette out of here. Robinson will be looking for both of you." Before Nash could protest, Cullen continued, "You're not in any shape to be fighting. Not yet anyway, and certainly not the way Robinson will. Plus, if you're hurt, who will take care of Jeanette?"

He ignored the narrow-eyed glare the lady sent him from behind Nash. Cullen couldn't help wondering what else he'd missed in his determination to avoid any sort of relationship or friendship. How had he not known Jeanette wasn't human? Why hadn't he figured out that Carter knew about the shifters and the pack?

None of it mattered right now. Shouts were coming from the parking lot and he had to get back out there to help Carter. He liked the sheriff, and once the pack got going, Carter would be hard-pressed to keep from getting seriously hurt.

"Get out of here, both of you. I don't want to have to worry about your safety while I'm dealing with those idiots out there."

Cullen spun around on his heels and raced out into the parking lot. Carter was down and several of the wolves were kicking at him. Robinson stood, cheering them on and taunting the sheriff.

Not waiting for an invitation, Cullen waded into the middle of the crowd, tossing men away like they were ragdolls. There wasn't a wolf among the pack that could come close to Cullen's strength. Not even Robinson, and that was why Robinson had hated Cullen ever since he'd arrived in Fallen Creek.

He didn't have time to assess the sheriff's injuries, so he scooped him up. After clearing a path to the side of the building, he laid Carter on the ground up against the wall and stood in front of him.

Cullen propped his fists on his hips and glared at the pack, amazingly still in human form, spread out in a semicircle in front of him. Some of them dropped their gazes and almost tilted their heads in a show of submission.

Most of them had meth or some other drug running through their blood, and they didn't have any control over their actions. Not that Cullen had expected them to do anything different. The men in Robinson's pack were cowards for the most part, especially those who'd gotten hooked on the drugs they were selling.

Cullen showed his fangs. He wasn't going to let them hurt Carter any more. The sheriff was just doing his job, trying to protect the humans in Fallen Creek. Cullen snarled, daring them to make a move toward him.

"Why are you doing this?" Robinson demanded.

He lifted his gaze from the followers to Robinson, standing behind them, far enough away that Cullen couldn't reach him.

Cullen shrugged. "I guess I just like fucking with you."

"I thought I told you to not interfere with me or my pack," Robinson reminded him.

"Oh, you did, but when you start messing with people I like, you mess with me." Cullen crossed his arms over his chest and glared at the Alpha. "You are starting to piss me off, Robinson, and you know what happens when I get pissed."

Robinson snorted, but he didn't move any closer. "Whatever, man. We have business with Jeanette and that new bartender of hers." Robinson slapped the shoulders of four of his guys. "You come with me. You others, take care of the lone wolf."

The five left didn't look happy about having to take Cullen on, but they were completely under Robinson's rule, so they would do as they were told.

Cullen didn't wait for them to come to him. He allowed his wolf to take over and his claws popped from his knuckles. With quick swings, he incapacitated two of them before they could even think about attacking him.

The other three shifted and launched themselves at him. Even without fully turning, he was still faster and stronger than they were. They fought like the animals they were inside. Howls and yelps filled the air as they took turns trying to get to him. Cullen made sure his back stayed toward the wall, his body between them and Carter.

"Oh hell, no!"

He looked over to where Nash was striding across the parking lot. There was rage in the man's face, but no shock at seeing Cullen being attacked by three wolves or at the fact that Cullen had claws.

One of the wolves whirled around and headed toward Nash. Cullen wasn't going to let the man get hurt. With all the injuries Nash was recovering from, Cullen knew the bartender wouldn't be able to take too much of a beating.

Cullen grabbed one of the wolves and slammed it against the wall. It yelped and slid to the ground. He kicked it to the side, not wanting it anywhere near Carter or Nash. The second wolf jumped on his back, sinking its teeth into his shoulder.

"Fuck!" he roared as he buried his claws into the wolf's back and flung it onto the ground.

Before he realized he'd made the decision, Cullen had torn the wolf's throat out. There would be no mercy from him, not anymore. For whatever reason, his wolf had decided it was time to assert itself and take what it wanted.

One of those things was the pack. Cullen's wolf was stronger than Robinson, and that meant it wanted to be the Alpha of the pack. Also, for some strange reason, his wolf had claimed Nash as his as well. It wanted the human and wasn't going to take no for an answer.

It knew they had to make it through the fight first, and

it would kill any wolf that got in its way. Eventually, he would have to face Robinson, but the fight wouldn't happen that night. Once Robinson realized his wolves had been defeated, he'd run until he could gather the rest of his pack, then he'd be back to take on Cullen.

"Take that, you furry motherfucker. I don't know where you came from, but I won't have you trying to hurt a woman on my watch."

Cullen turned from where he'd crouched over the dead shifter, and he saw Nash kicking the shit out of a wolf lying on the ground in front of him. Cullen winced at the force of those steel-toed boots hitting the wolf's side.

"Nash, stop. If he's not dead, he's going to wish he was when he wakes up."

Nash glanced up, his eyes wild and filled with rage. "I don't fucking care. He fucking attacked you and was going to hurt Jeanette. Wait, does he have rabies or something? Why would he attack you like that?"

"Ummm…" Cullen looked back at the dead wolf lying in the shadows over by Carter. "Robinson trained them as attack dogs. He wanted something more vicious than a pit bull."

He winced but hoped Nash was too caught up in beating the shit out of the wolf to notice that Cullen had torn the throat out of the other one with his bare hands. Something like that was hard to explain to a potential lover, along with the whole 'I'm a wolf shifter' thing. Those types of talks never went well.

"Should we go after Robinson and the others? They've probably trashed Jeanette's bar by now." Nash's entire body shook with anger.

Cullen approached with caution, not wanting to freak the man out, and he also kept a tight grip on his wolf. The beast wanted to take Nash down and claim him as his own, which would be even more difficult to explain than all the other stuff combined.

Chapter Five

Nash watched as Cullen stalked toward him. There was something in the way the man moved that caused shivers to run down Nash's spine. They were tremors of lust mixed with a sliver of fear. Cullen moved like he was hunting Nash.

There was a gleam in Cullen's eyes Nash had seen in other men's gazes. Usually it was the men of the club looking at their women that way. Possessive desire shone on Cullen's face and it made Nash hard. He'd never thought some guy staring at him like he was the cherry on top of the sundae would turn him on.

"Yes, we probably should go inside. Carter called for backup before the whole thing went to shit, so the other deputies should be arriving soon."

As he spoke, the sound of sirens began to reach them, and relief surged through Nash. His ribs and the rest of his body were killing him, and while he wouldn't back away from a fight, he didn't know how much longer he could take a beating.

"Looks like the cavalry's about to arrive, but I still need to go inside," Cullen said, frowning at the wolf at Nash's feet. "I have to talk to Robinson."

"Why? Why warn him that the police are coming?"

"It's not to warn him about the police. It's to challenge him. I need to let him know that I'm not going to take this shit anymore." Cullen shoved his hand through his hair.

Nash stared at Cullen. It looked like the man had more hair than usual. And his teeth... It seemed like Cullen had fangs.

"What shit? And why now? You've been here for a while. What makes tonight different?" Nash tilted his head. "What are you going to do to Robinson, if you aren't going to let the police handle it?"

Cullen pushed into Nash's personal space and leaned down to crush his lips against Nash's. He wrapped his arms around Cullen's shoulders, opening his mouth to Cullen's demand for entrance. Their tongues dueled and teased with each stroke.

Nash forgot about his aches and pains. He forgot about the wolves lying on the ground around him. All he focused on was the way Cullen embraced him, bringing their bodies together.

Nash moaned low in his throat, wanting more than just kisses. He wanted Cullen to shove him against a wall and take him hard and fast. He didn't want gentleness or tenderness. As the adrenaline pulsed through his body, Nash couldn't see any reason why having sex with Cullen wouldn't be a good idea.

It didn't matter that he wasn't planning on sticking around Fallen Creek, or even that he didn't know anything about the man. Hell, he'd fucked guys whose names he'd never known. There was something about Cullen that was driving Nash into throwing all his caution to the wind.

The sound of tires on the gravel of the parking lot broke them up.

"Shit!" Cullen took two huge steps away from Nash. "I didn't mean to do that."

"It's all right. Your blood's up and I was close." Nash squashed the disappointment trying to rear its head in his chest.

"That's not really what I meant, but I don't have time to tell you what I was thinking." Cullen took off, racing to the entrance of the bar. "I need to talk to Robinson."

Nash dashed after Cullen, not wanting the man to go into the bar without backup. Of course, Cullen didn't seem to need his help, considering he'd been taking on three wolves on his own before Nash had shown up. But Nash wasn't the type of guy to let a friend go in outnumbered.

"Robinson," Cullen shouted after shoving the door open.

Glancing around the room, Nash felt his rage rise again. The entire bar was trashed. Tables and chairs had been destroyed and there were broken bottles all over the floor.

Robinson whirled around and stared at Cullen. Nash blinked, sure he wasn't seeing what he thought he saw. Robinson's eyes were glowing and his teeth were elongated like the huge canines of a dog—or wolf.

"What do you want?" Robinson snarled, sticking his chest out and puffing up.

Nash bit back his laughter. There was no way the man could even dream of being able to fight Cullen and win. He was shorter and thinner than Cullen. Also, if Nash wasn't crazy, it looked like Robinson had started to sample his own product, too, which was never a good idea for a drug dealer.

"I'm here to tell you it's over. All your bullshit and fucking drug dealing are done." Cullen glared at Robinson and propped his fists on his hips.

Robinson snorted. "Who's going to stop me? You?"

"Yes."

In the time it took Cullen to say the three-letter word, Nash saw fear blossom in Robinson's eyes. Robinson stiffened and all the others in the room froze. Nash didn't know what was going on, but he did get the feeling that what Cullen had said was far more serious than what it had sounded like.

The tension in the bar grew as Cullen and Robinson stared at each other. Nash wasn't sure whether he should go farther in or hang out by the door. Finally, Robinson nodded.

"All right. Tomorrow night at the ring. You know the rules, though I'm not sure who you'll bring as your seconds." Robinson snorted. "These humans are frail creatures and easily broken if hit hard enough. They can't help you rule the pack."

"I don't need seconds. No one in your pack is strong enough to take me down. All I need to do is kill you and then they're mine."

Nash blinked and shook his head. He hadn't just heard Cullen tell Robinson he was going to kill him? There was something odd going on and Nash wasn't sure if he wanted to know what all the underlying currents meant.

"Fine. We'll end this in the ring. I'll see you at dark tomorrow night." Robinson curled his lip and what light was left in the bar shone on his teeth.

This time Nash knew what he was seeing was real. Robinson had fangs and elongated canines. The gang leader's eyes took on a red tint and Nash swore the man seemed bigger somehow.

Of course, when Nash looked at Cullen, he noticed the same thing. Cullen's shirt struggled to cover the man's shoulders and the seams of his jeans stretched like Cullen was growing bigger each second.

If danger had a feel or scent, it would be filling this room, Nash thought, as the very air weighed heavily on his shoulders. He'd been in dangerous situations before while working as the sergeant-at-arms for his motorcycle club, but some instinct buried deep inside told him the trouble brewing in this bar was far different. It felt far more deadly than anything he'd been involved with before. *Damn it. I thought I'd gotten away from this. How did I manage to run into a pack in such an out-of-the-way place?*

"The police are outside. They'll be coming through the door any minute now. I suggest you give yourselves up quietly, then you might get out by tomorrow night." Cullen laughed harshly. "You know what the consequences are for not appearing at a challenge fight."

"You don't have to explain the laws to me, O'Murphy. I'll be there, and you'll find out just how weak a lone wolf is against the might of a true Alpha." Robinson snarled.

Cullen shrugged, and Nash could see how unaffected

by Robinson's threat the man was. Stepping to one side, Nash watched as Robinson's gang filed out of the building. Robinson brought up the rear and growled at Nash as he passed him.

A warning rumble emerged from Cullen, causing Robinson to straighten and move past Nash without further incident. Nash didn't watch them leave, keeping his gaze on Cullen, who stood in the middle of the bar with his hands clenched.

Cullen's chest heaved as he took in deep breaths, like he was trying to control his anger. Yet Nash never got the feeling Cullen was in danger of losing control. He edged closer and Cullen raised his head, his eyes gleaming red like Robinson's had been.

"What the hell are you?" Nash reached out to rest his hand on Cullen's broad chest.

The man's heart raced under Nash's palm and when their eyes met, he saw need flare in Cullen's. He knew there was an answering response in his.

"I want to kiss you right now," Cullen whispered, his voice sounding like he'd swallowed glass.

"I want you to do more than that," Nash confessed, "but we have a group of deputies out there who are going to want to talk to us. You're going to have to explain how you managed to kill that one wolf without giving anything away about yourself."

"What's there to give away? I sliced his throat with a rock that I threw away before I came in here."

The look Cullen gave Nash was very practiced and innocent and full of bullshit. Nash knew it, but he also understood the underlying message. Nothing would be said about how the wolf had died or how Cullen had managed to kill a full-grown wolf with his bare hands. As far as the police were concerned, Cullen had had some kind of weapon.

"I'd like to discuss this whole situation when we're alone," Nash warned Cullen.

The cowboy snorted. "Do you really think we'll be talking when I can get you somewhere private?"

He shuddered as lust tore through him. "All right. We'll talk about everything after we fuck."

Cullen leaned closer, and Nash inhaled sharply as Cullen's hot breath washed over his ear.

"You mean after I fuck you into the mattress, right?"

Nash gulped. No man had ever talked to him like that. Normally, they assumed he would be the one fucking them. A little bit of fear wound through his excitement.

He wasn't a small guy by any means, but Cullen towered over him by several inches, and, glancing down, Nash could tell Cullen was big all over. Nash had never bottomed in all the years he'd been fucking.

His cock hardened and he moaned as the pain of his zipper pressing into his hot flesh shot through him. *Christ!* Talking to the cops better not take long, or he was going to come in his jeans just at the thought of Cullen's cock in his virgin ass.

"Mr. O'Murphy, Sheriff Carter is asking for you."

They turned to look at the deputy standing just inside the door. How long had he been standing there? Had he heard anything of what Cullen had said to Nash?

Cullen strolled over to the man before saying, "So he's conscious?"

"Barely, and they want to take him to the hospital right now, but he won't let them until he talks to you." The officer was younger than Nash and Cullen and he kept his gaze on the floor, almost like he knew meeting Cullen's gaze was forbidden.

"Fine." Cullen glanced over his shoulder at Nash. "Come with me."

It wasn't a request, but Nash didn't argue. He simply joined them at the entrance and let Cullen leave first.

They followed the deputy over to Carter, who struggled against the EMTs, not letting them put him in the back of the ambulance.

"Stop it, Carter. I'm here." Cullen pushed through the other policemen and grabbed Carter's arm.

"Are you going to take care of this?" Carter's voice held pain and anger.

"Yes."

At the single word from Cullen, Carter calmed down and the EMTs took him away. They answered all the deputies' questions before they were allowed to go.

Again, Nash stayed quiet as they made their way over to Cullen's truck. Cullen opened the passenger door before turning to look at him.

"You know what will happen if you come back to my ranch with me."

Nash nodded.

"It's up to you. If you don't want this, you can go back to your trailer and I won't bring it up again." Cullen narrowed his eyes and raked his glaze over Nash from his head to his feet. "Though I'll be extremely disappointed if you choose to return to your trailer."

Nash took a moment and thought about it. Fucking Cullen wouldn't be like his usual hook-ups. It would end up with him getting his ass fucked by the rancher. Somehow, the thought of bottoming didn't upset him nearly as much as he might once have thought it would.

He took a deep breath and climbed into the truck. Nash put his seatbelt on while Cullen walked around to the driver's side. Rubbing his suddenly sweaty palms on his jeans, Nash watched Cullen stop and stretch.

The way the muscles flexed under the man's shirt caught Nash's attention and he realized just how attracted he was to Cullen, more so than any other man he'd been with.

Cullen got into the truck and they pulled out of the parking lot. Nash didn't pay attention to where they were going. He simply reached out and rested his hand on Cullen's leg.

He stroked along the seam of Cullen's jeans up to the bulge between his thighs. He pressed his palm against it and Cullen grunted. Tightening his grip, he rubbed and squeezed until Cullen was lifting and thrusting his hips.

"Open my jeans. I don't want to come in them like a teenager." Cullen's command grated out of his throat.

Nash chuckled but did as he was told. He somehow managed to get Cullen's belt open and the button and zipper undone without letting go of Cullen. They both groaned as Nash slid his hand beneath the denim of Cullen's pants and surrounded the man's cock.

"Fuck. You're so thick. You're going to tear me up," Nash noted as he pumped.

"I'll take care of you and make sure it's good. I want you to beg me to fuck you." Cullen gripped the steering wheel, his knuckles turning white.

"Pull over," Nash told Cullen, wanting more than his hand on the hot, hard flesh Cullen was packing.

The tires of the truck screeched as Cullen slammed on the brakes and threw the vehicle into park on the side of the road. Nash unhooked his seatbelt and gestured for Cullen to move his seat back.

As soon as it was done, Nash swooped in and wrapped his lips around the flared head of Cullen's cock. Cullen fisted his hand in his hair, holding him in place. Nash hadn't given many blow jobs in his life. In fact, he was usually the one getting them, but he discovered he wanted to feel Cullen's cock on his tongue and in his mouth.

"Take your time, Nash. I know I'm a lot to get used to, but I think you can do it. Don't go all the way down until you're ready." Cullen massaged the back of Nash's head, encouraging him with his voice but not forcing him to do anything.

Nash encircled the base of Cullen's cock and stroked up as he took more of it in his mouth. He moved up and down, applying as much suction as he could, while he jerked Cullen off as well.

"Shit! I knew the moment I saw you, you'd be good at this," Cullen muttered. "Your mouth was meant to be fucked."

Nash rolled his eyes and gave a mental snort. He'd said the same thing to several of his fucks. It was just a line, yet something about those words and the desire in Cullen's voice make Nash's cock stiffen even more.

He kept up his pleasuring of Cullen, fumbling with the fastening of his jeans. He hummed around the shaft in his mouth as he fisted his cock and started jerking off.

"I can't wait to get you home and get your cock in my mouth."

A little bit of surprise rang through Nash. He hadn't thought Cullen would be the type of guy who would give a blow job. There was something very dominant about Cullen, and the men Nash knew who were like that wouldn't be caught dead pleasuring a person — woman or man — except by fucking them.

Cullen caressed Nash's hollowed cheek. "You seemed shocked by my wanting that. Alpha men don't do anything that makes them appear weak in the eyes of others."

Nash nodded slightly, not stopping what he was doing. He must not be doing it right if Cullen could still make sense like that.

"Don't worry, Nash. I'll pleasure you with my mouth, hand and cock. If it lasts long enough, I might even let you fuck me. I believe giving my lover a climax and making sure he's happy is the most important thing I can do. It makes me a real man, in my opinion."

Tingling built at the base of Nash's spine, but he was determined to make Cullen come before he did. He sped up, and soon Cullen was gently fucking his mouth, making sure Nash didn't gag.

"I'm going to come," Cullen warned.

It wasn't the smartest thing, but Nash wanted to taste Cullen and he was willing to take the risk. If he'd been in a city, or anywhere else for that matter, he would've been using a condom. Yet something told him Cullen would've mentioned it if they'd needed to be extra careful.

A loud grunt filled the truck's cab and salty cum flooded

his mouth. He swallowed each spurt, savoring the bitterness of Cullen's seed. Cullen thrust his cock in and out of Nash's mouth until every last drop coated his tongue and throat.

Only when Cullen stopped moving did Nash lick the man's cock clean and pull away. He flopped back into his seat, breathing hard while rubbing his palm over his hard-on. Whimpering, he wasn't sure if he should finish getting himself off now, or wait until they got to Cullen's ranch and let Cullen fuck him until he came.

"Stop touching yourself," Cullen ordered in a harsh voice.

Nash froze and shot Cullen an incredulous look. "What the hell? Are you seriously telling me what to do?"

Cullen's gaze pinned him to the seat. "Yes, I am. Anticipation will build, and when I finally fuck that tight ass of yours, it'll blow your mind."

"Shit!" Nash swore as his cock stiffened even more and began to ache with need. "You're not my boss."

"Maybe not out in the world, but in bed, I will be."

"This time, but don't expect me to bottom every time."

He jerked as Cullen grabbed his hand and pulled it away from his crotch. Nash didn't fight, not like he would normally do if someone manhandled him like that. While Cullen's grip was tight, Nash had the feeling he would let go if Nash asked him to do so.

The grin on Cullen's face told Nash he knew Nash would yield that night. Yet there was also something shining in Cullen's eyes that said they would have another discussion the next time they fucked.

"We'll come back to that later. Now, keep your hands away from your dick and I'll get us to my place without causing an accident."

Nodding, Nash rested his hands on the dashboard. He'd do what Cullen wanted for the moment. Mostly because it really excited him to be told what to do instead of being the one giving the orders. He was really turned on by the growl in Cullen's voice.

"Since I can't get off, and you've already come, what am

I supposed to do? I know, we can play Twenty Questions."

Cullen merely grunted. Nash smiled to himself.

"What the hell was that whole confrontation thing back at the bar? Why is it a big deal that you're challenging Robinson? I saw how the man looked at you. He's scared of you." Nash shook his head.

"Robinson is scared of me because he knows I can beat him. He doesn't want to lose control of the pack, and that's what's going to happen tomorrow night." Cullen frowned and slammed his fist against the steering wheel. "I waited too long. I should've done this earlier, but I thought I could stay out of the affairs of this town."

"Why would you not want to get involved? Aren't they your friends?" He blinked at the glare Cullen shot him. "What did I say?"

"I don't have friends, Rhodes. I'm a lone wolf, and I've always preferred to stay that way, until you showed up and threw a wrench in my plans. To be honest, I didn't care what Robinson was doing. He wasn't bothering me and it's no skin off my nose if humans are destroying their lives with the meth Robinson's gang cooks."

"Humans? What exactly do you mean by that? I heard Robinson say something about humans in the bar, too."

Cullen snarled at Nash's questions but didn't answer them. Nash reached over before punching Cullen in the arm.

"What secrets are you hiding? Are you some kind of alien or something?" His hand rebounded off Cullen's iron-like biceps. Nash shook it. "Shit, man. What are you made of, steel?"

"No. I'm not an alien or made of steel. I'm just a guy who knows how I can take Robinson out of the equation and free Fallen Creek from his reign."

"Why not just go to the police and get them to arrest Robinson?" Nash didn't understand why Cullen wasn't heading straight to the police, not that Nash had wanted to be around any lawman at any time in his life.

Cullen took a deep breath before speaking. "I can't let them get a hold of Robinson. There are things about Robinson the world isn't ready to discover, and it's up to me to keep them from finding out all of the facts."

Nash snorted. "You're talking in riddles, man. I'm not sure what's going on, but I plan on finding out."

"You can try." Cullen looked at him quickly before returning his gaze to the road. "I think you should be putting your energy toward deciding how many times you want me to fuck you tonight."

"How many times do you think you can get it up, old man?"

"Old man? You didn't seriously just call me that."

Nash chuckled. "I did, because I'm pretty sure you're older than me."

Cullen laughed. "You have no idea, Rhodes."

Nash rubbed his hand over Cullen's thigh, drawing a muffled groan from the man, followed by a deep growl. He gave Cullen a very innocent look.

"What? You said I couldn't touch myself. You didn't say anything about me touching you."

"Just be careful. You don't know just what you're getting yourself into by teasing me. I might have to punish you when we get to my place. You might not be able to walk tomorrow."

Humming, Nash suppressed the shudder trying to race around his body. God, he couldn't wait to get to Cullen's and let the man have at his ass. It wasn't something he'd ever done before, but hell, every second that passed made him more than willing to bend over and take whatever Cullen gave him.

Was that how the men Nash had slept with felt? Had they been as excited as he was, or had they simply been unwilling to say no to him because of his reputation in the club? His anticipation waned slightly. Nash hated the thought that his former lovers had only slept with him because they'd worried he'd do something to them.

He'd never hurt innocent people. His reluctance to do so had been a bone of contention with the gang.

"You're thinking really hard over there all of a sudden." Cullen broke through his thoughts.

"Nothing important. How much farther to your place?" He didn't want to talk about his past.

"Only about another mile or so."

Nash let silence fill the cab while he worked on getting his lust back on track.

Chapter Six

Cullen pulled up in front of his house and turned the truck off. He held onto the steering wheel for a moment, trying to decide if he was really going to take Nash to his bed. It was one thing to have a one-off in the bathroom of a club in the city. It was entirely a different thing to fuck some guy he could run into every day for the rest of his life, at least until Nash left in a couple of weeks.

"Are you having second thoughts?"

He jerked when Nash's question broke through his musing. Cullen turned to look at the human. Doubt skipped over Nash's face and Cullen wondered if Nash was having second thoughts as well. Maybe he'd come on too strong. Maybe Nash wasn't willing to bottom for him.

If that were the case, would Cullen be able to accept someone else fucking him? His wolf growled inside him and he acknowledged it might never happen.

"No. Just trying to remember if I made the bed this morning before I left."

Nash snorted. "I don't think it matters, man. It's not like we're not going to mess it up when you screw me."

Well, that answered his questions. Cullen took the keys out of the ignition and opened the truck door. He gestured for Nash to join him at the front of the vehicle.

"So you're okay with me fucking you? Is it the first time for you?"

He needed to know so he could take it slow for him.

"Yes." Nash ducked his head, but somehow Cullen knew he was blushing.

"Thanks for being honest. I'll do my best to make it good

for you."

After unlocking the front door, Cullen stepped back and waved Nash inside. He breathed deeply as the man walked past him. Cullen barely swallowed the howl his wolf wanted to send up at the scent of desire rolling off Nash.

"I have to go and feed the animals before we can do anything. You want to hang out here? There's beer in the fridge and there's probably some food in there as well." He rubbed his hand over his face and sighed.

"Can I go with you? I'll help out when I can, as long as you tell me what to do." Nash grinned. "I've never been on a ranch before."

"Where are you from?"

They walked through the house and out of the back door to the barns. Cullen gave Nash instructions as they went through feeding and watering the horses. The cattle would be fine for the night. He'd ride out in the morning to check on them.

He didn't really pay close attention to what Nash was telling him about being from Nashville and why he was on his way out to Santa Monica to visit his mother. He was trying to figure out how to deal with another person in his home, being used to solitude. Having someone else helping him with chores made them go by faster, yet Cullen wasn't sure he really liked having someone in his personal space. Not even when his wolf couldn't seem to get close enough to Nash. If he didn't have absolute control over the beast, he'd have Nash pinned in a corner of one of the stalls while his wolf sniffed and licked the man everywhere.

He brushed up against Nash every chance he could get. Each time Nash leaned into his touch, Cullen's cock stiffened. Cullen rushed through the last feeding and when they'd finished, he grabbed Nash by the hand, dragging the man behind him.

His wolf wasn't going to be able to wait much longer to take Nash. If he believed all the bullshit romance books, he'd think Nash was his mate. Since there wasn't anything like mates in the wolf shifter world, he wasn't worried about what would happen when they did fuck. It would be easy to watch Nash walk out of his life when the man decided to leave.

Cullen didn't stop until they were in the bedroom. He shut the door behind them before turning to push Nash up against the wall. His movements were careful because even in the wave of desire and lust washing over him, he remembered that Nash was still nursing injuries from before.

He crushed their lips together, demanding entrance to Nash's mouth while he ripped Nash's shirt off his body. Cullen let the strips of fabric fall to the floor at their feet. Nash buried his hands in Cullen's hair, hanging onto him as tightly as possible.

Cullen sucked on Nash's bottom lip, nipping at the man's flesh. He growled when Nash moaned and arched into his pelvis. The feel of Nash's erection grinding into his was causing his control to break.

Nash sucked in his stomach when Cullen slid his hands into the waistband of Nash's jeans and struggled with the button and zipper. When he got those undone, he shoved the edges of the fabric down, along with Nash's underwear.

He dropped, not even noticing the pain when his knees connected with the floor. After wrapping his hand around Nash's cock, Cullen brought it to his mouth and sucked it in.

"Holy shit!"

A thud reached his ears and he glanced up to see Nash had his eyes closed and his head was resting against the door. Cullen took Nash in as far as he could, until his nose was buried in the man's pubic hair.

"I didn't think you'd do this." Nash's voice sounded strained.

Cullen pulled out and rocked back on his heels. "Just because I'm going to fuck you doesn't mean I don't like giving head. I like the feel of a guy's cock in my mouth."

"I didn't say to stop what you're doing, man." Nash waved his trembling hand at his dick.

Cullen chuckled. "All right. I'll let you be the boss at the moment."

He didn't wait to hear what Nash had to say. He bent forward and took Nash's cock back into his mouth. He swirled his tongue around the fleshy glans, tasting the pre-cum leaking from the slit. Cullen bobbed up and down, applying suction as he did so.

He also stroked his hand along the hot flesh, bringing it up to meet his lips each time. Nash jerked and Cullen tapped the man's thigh, letting him know it was okay to move.

Cullen grunted when Nash gripped the back of his head and began thrusting his hips, driving his cock as deep into Cullen's mouth as he could without choking him. Cullen let Nash do as he pleased while he slipped one of his fingers into his mouth alongside Nash's cock.

After getting it nice and wet, he slid it around to Nash's butt and rubbed the tip over his puckered ring. Nash moaned, pushing back against his finger. Cullen hummed around the hard flesh in his mouth, trying to tell his lover to be careful.

It being Nash's first time, Cullen didn't want to him to hurt himself by moving too fast. Each time he slipped a little farther in, not forcing Nash to take all of his finger at once.

When he'd sunk all the way in, he twisted his finger and brushed against Nash's gland.

"Holy fuck!" Nash jerked and thrust like he wasn't sure which way he should move.

Cullen caressed Nash's hip, soothing him, before gripping his body and encouraging him to keep moving. He knew the combination of his fingers and his mouth would get Nash off, plus he could get the man stretched for when he fucked him.

"Damn. I'm gonna come, Cullen," Nash warned him.

He took his hand off Nash's cock and grabbed both of Nash's butt cheeks. Cullen opened his mouth as wide as possible, taking every inch that he could. Nash moved faster and faster. His grunts surrounded Cullen, letting him know how much Nash was enjoying what he was doing to him.

Cullen allowed his teeth to gently scrape over the soft skin covering Nash's hard-on while hitting his gland and pushed Nash over the edge into his climax.

Nash threw his head back, bouncing it against the door several times as he jerked. Cullen drank down all the cum spilling from Nash's cock. It was the weirdest thing — Nash's seed was the best he'd ever tasted, even though it was bitter and salty.

He sucked and licked until Nash stopped moving and slumped back. Cullen eased off, removing his finger as well. Without saying a word, he surged to his feet, scooped Nash over his shoulder and carried him to the bed.

After tossing Nash on the mattress, Cullen stripped himself. Nash lay there, blinking slowly, like he was trying to sort things out. Cullen quickly tore the rest of Nash's clothes off, tossing them over his shoulder, not caring where the things landed.

He scrambled through his nightstand, looking for the lube and condoms. He didn't have to worry about diseases from Nash, but since Nash didn't know that, he had to make it look good.

"Got it," he shouted, before pouncing on the mattress.

Cullen crawled between Nash's legs, tearing the foil package and getting the rubber out. He rolled it onto his erection, humming at the lust shooting through him at the touch of his own hand.

He squirted lube onto his palm before slicking up his cock. Putting more on his fingers, he looked up at Nash. The man stared at him with a touch of worry in his eyes.

"Don't be afraid. I'll make sure this is good for you and it'll only hurt a little. I can't take it all away."

Nash took a deep breath. "I know. Just do it now while I'm still relaxed."

Cullen pushed his fingers in and started stretching Nash again, lubing him up. He didn't take as long this time, needing to be inside Nash as soon as possible.

Nash's legs went over Cullen's shoulders and he positioned the head of his cock at Nash's opening. He breached the ring of muscle slow and easy, not wanting to rush anything.

"Fuck," Nash said, drawing the word out as Cullen sank deeper into him.

Finally, Cullen bottomed out and he froze. Their gazes met, and Nash's eyes were wide.

"Are you all right?" Cullen managed to ask.

Nash actually seemed to think about it, and Cullen respected him for that. Instead of nodding and letting Cullen go at him, he considered the question.

"It's a little weird, but I'm okay at the moment. You can move whenever you want."

"Oh, thank God. I couldn't stay still for much longer."

Cullen slipped his hands around Nash's shoulders and started pounding Nash's ass. Nash reached up, pressing his hands to the headboard to keep from being pushed into it. Cullen was intent on fucking Nash as hard as he could.

"Oh, man. Christ! You're so fucking huge. Shit! I'm going to come again."

Blinking at Nash's words, Cullen peeled one of his hands from Nash's shoulder to reach down and wrap it around Nash's cock. He gripped it tightly but allowed his own thrusts to move Nash's erection through his fingers.

He angled his hips a fraction of an inch, which rubbed the head of his cock over Nash's gland with every movement. Tingling swelled at the base of Cullen's spine, alerting him to the fact his own climax was close.

Speeding up, he slammed into Nash. "Come on, Nash. Cover my hand with your spunk."

Nash shouted and warm liquid spilled over Cullen's

fingers. It was the scent of Nash's orgasm that yanked Cullen's from him. He threw back his head and howled as he flooded the condom.

They trembled and shuddered together, encouraging the last drops from each other. Nash winced as Cullen's softened cock slipped from his ass. Cullen grabbed the condom and rolled off the bed, wandering to the bathroom to clean up. He wet a cloth and took it out to wash Nash off.

He tossed the dirty cloth toward the other room and curled up with Nash under the covers.

"I've never had anyone clean me off like that," Nash spoke.

Cullen frowned, wondering why what he'd done was worth mentioning. He often cleaned up after having sex or even jacking off. As much as his wolf loved the scent of sex, the human part of Cullen didn't like it, and he rarely allowed his wolf to have control. Also, he didn't enjoy smelling like other men, though he could see himself getting used to Nash's scent on his skin. And didn't that thought freak him out a little.

"Sorry. If you don't want me to do it, I won't."

Nash chuckled, sleep evident in his tone. "No big deal, man. It's just different. I rarely stay in bed with a man. Once we both got off, I'd head home. Easier than risk getting caught leaving a guy's apartment the next morning."

"The people you're used to hanging out with not big on gays?"

Nash's snort of disbelief shook them both. "Dude, they aren't big on anything that isn't white, straight and male. I was always glad I could pass as straight."

"You mean what we see on those TV shows isn't real?" Cullen had always wondered about that. Of course, nothing on TV or in the movies about shifters was true, so he shouldn't be surprised if the rest of the shit was wrong as well.

"Oh, I think it's about fifty-fifty on whether it's right or not. Some writers get closer than others. Just depends on the club and the guys in it." Nash rolled over onto his back and he stroked his hand up and down Cullen's arm, which lay on his stomach. He stared up at the ceiling.

Cullen studied the man lying next to him. It had been a long time since he'd allowed anyone to share his bed. It wasn't that he didn't want to sleep with another man, but being an Alpha wolf meant he hated sharing his territory with anyone else. Yet there was something about Nash that Cullen's wolf accepted.

"Your club is full of chauvinistic assholes," Cullen stated.

"Most of them are. The ones who aren't don't speak up. It's not worth getting a beat-down for protesting against custom. I'm not proud of the fact that I turned my back several times to avoid confrontations."

Cullen caressed the warm skin under his fingers. "We all do things we hate in order to protect ourselves. It doesn't make you a bad guy because you chose to save yourself. I've done it more in my lifetime than most."

"Yet you're going to fight Robinson to stop his reign of terror. Sounds to me like you're risking your life for the people of Fallen Creek." Nash turned his gaze on Cullen and there was a questioning light in his eyes.

"Not for the people of Fallen Creek. I'm doing it specifically for Jeanette."

And for Nash, but Cullen wasn't going to say that out loud. He didn't think Nash would appreciate Cullen doing something to protect him. Nash struck him as being an independent kind of guy who thought he could take care of himself. If Robinson were a run-of-the-mill drug dealer, Cullen wouldn't have even considered stepping into the middle of the shit storm. But Robinson wasn't the ordinary kind of crazy and Cullen was the only person who could stop him.

Well, Jeanette might have been able to do it, if she'd been inclined to. Cullen still hadn't figured out what she was, knowing only that she was neither human nor wolf. Why hadn't she stepped up either? Why was she as reluctant as

Cullen to take Robinson out?

He'd have to go and ask her in the morning. Nash would want to go back to town and help clean up the bar. Cullen's plans involved making sure his animals were okay before shifting and spending most of the day as a wolf, getting in touch with his beast. It helped his fighting skills when he was as close to his animal as possible. Cullen had no illusion that Robinson wouldn't cheat somehow. Cullen would just have to try to be one step ahead of the other Alpha all the time.

"Don't you have any family around here?" Nash's low question surprised Cullen and he jerked.

"My family is dead. It was just my parents and me, and we moved around a lot, so I never had time to make friends." Cullen paused and thought for a moment before continuing, "I think this is the longest I've ever stayed in one place. I've been here for four years or so."

"Seriously?" Nash looked incredulous. "I can't imagine moving that often. Hell, I've lived in Nashville all my life."

Cullen lifted one shoulder slightly. "When all you've done your whole life is move, it's not that hard to keep up the pattern. But I like it out here."

Nash rolled on his side, facing Cullen, and smiled. "I can kind of see why you'd like it out here. Aside from Robinson and his gang, the other townspeople seem nice, though I don't have a lot of experience with nice people. I tend to run with the wild and angry crowd. Or at least, I did back home. Maybe it's time to turn over a new leaf."

"I'm not sure how wild and angry they are out in Santa Monica. You could always join the surfer crowd. There might still be drugs involved, but maybe nothing like meth."

Cullen didn't really know anything about the West Coast. He'd never been out there because his parents had tended to stay in less populated areas to avoid wolf packs.

"You're right. Maybe surfing can be my new drug of choice, instead of riding my bike all over the place." Nash didn't look very convinced.

It didn't really matter whether Nash thought surfing would be more fun than riding his bike. It wasn't like Cullen would be there to watch the man surf anyway. Once he beat Robinson, he was stuck running the Fallen Creek pack and he wouldn't be going anywhere ever again.

After settling back, Cullen pulled Nash tight against his chest and closed his eyes. He tried not to think about the upcoming fight or what would happen when Nash left Fallen Creek. All that was important was to absorb the feeling of another being in his arms.

He didn't know how long he'd lain there before Nash's steady breathing informed him that his lover was asleep. He managed to untangle himself from Nash's arms and slide out of bed. After padding out of his bedroom, he made his way down the hallway to the kitchen.

Standing in front of the sink, he stared out of the window. All the barns and cattle as far as he could see were his, and for the first time, he didn't want to leave. He'd never wanted to put down roots or become so attached to anything or anyone that he wouldn't want to leave them behind when the time came.

He'd been in Fallen Creek for four years, and, while he hadn't been the friendliest of people, he had managed to make some acquaintances. Had his father ever longed to stay somewhere long enough to make friends? Had his mother wished for friends she could gossip with?

But look how the one time they had stuck around had ended. Sara's family had become very close friends of Cullen's family, and they'd spent a lot of time together in northern Minnesota. Sara had been his first friend and it hurt Cullen every time he thought about her.

He filled a glass with water before lifting it to his mouth, watching Nash stroll into the room. They were both naked and Cullen liked the way Nash was built. Every inch of the biker spoke of solidity, of confidence and possibly even loyalty. Yet how could Cullen really know that? He'd only known the man a couple of days, and already he was thinking in permanent terms with him.

"What happens if you don't win the fight?"

Cullen set the glass in the sink after emptying it. He turned to lean his ass against the counter. Crossing his arms over his chest, he met Nash's gaze. "Do you really think I can't win?"

Nash shook his head. "No. It's not that I don't think you'll win. It's just I think Robinson will cheat because he's a crazy bastard. I assume there are rules to this challenge."

"Yes." Cullen nodded.

The rules for challenging an Alpha had been written centuries ago and every wolf knew them. If Robinson broke any of the rules, his life was forfeit.

"I know there's something about this whole situation you're not telling me." Nash glared at him.

"I don't know what you're talking about." He kept his face expressionless, not wanting to give anything away.

Nash lifted one eyebrow with a skeptical look. "You do know what I'm talking about. Why not just call the state police and tell them what you know about Robinson's drug dealing? That would be the best way to get rid of him and his gang."

"Not all of Robinson's pack is bad. Some of them simply don't have a choice or are too afraid of him to stand up to him." Cullen ran his gaze over Nash, zeroing in on the man's groin. He licked his lips, wondering about getting a chance to wrap his lips around Nash's cock again.

Nash's dick twitched and, as Cullen continued to stare at it, it stiffened and lengthened. Before Cullen could push away from the counter and approach Nash, though, the biker had stalked across the room and dropped to the floor.

"What are you doing?"

He knew it was a stupid question, but his mind went blank when Nash fisted his cock and wrapped his mouth around it. Cullen let his head drop back and groaned as his shaft sank into a warm, moist space.

Cullen wasn't sure how often Nash gave blow jobs, so he tried not to thrust farther in without Nash letting him know it was all right. He braced his hands on the counter and spread his legs slightly.

Nash hummed as he slid his hands around Cullen's ass and gripped the firm flesh. He tapped one of Cullen's butt cheeks, and Cullen assumed he was saying he was ready for Cullen to move.

He slowly slid in and out of Nash's mouth, loving the feeling of suction around his cock. The way Nash pressed the tip of his tongue into the slit at the top of Cullen's cock was driving him crazy.

After slipping his hands into Nash's hair, Cullen held his head still while he fucked the man's mouth. Cullen's wolf loved the fact that Nash allowed him to take control of the situation. Also, his human hoped that by distracting Nash, they wouldn't have to talk about why Cullen couldn't bring the authorities in on the problem.

No way could any human find out about wolf shifters, though he'd have to talk to Carter and discover how the sheriff had figured out who they were.

When Nash fondled his balls, tugging on them slightly, Cullen's mind went blank again. There were more important things to think about at the moment. His climax built and the pressure grew under his skin until he couldn't contain it anymore.

He threw back his head and howled, flooding Nash's mouth with his cum. Nash choked a little bit, easing off so he could swallow all of what Cullen gave him.

Cullen trembled and moaned until Nash finished licking him clean.

Nash tugged at Cullen's fingers, trying to get him to release his hair. Cullen did before he sank to his knees. He pushed Nash over on his ass and dove down to swallow Nash's cock.

"Holy fuck!" Nash shouted and came, pouring his seed down Cullen's throat.

He drank every drop down, absorbing Nash's essence, until they both collapsed in a pile on the kitchen floor.

Chapter Seven

Nash stretched as he woke, wincing at the aches in parts of his body that had never been sore before. *What the hell?* He stared up at the ceiling, slowly recognizing it wasn't the same water-stained expanse he'd looked at each morning since he'd arrived in Fallen Creek.

No...this ceiling was off-white and there weren't any stains on it at all. The sheets covering his naked body were soft and far more expensive than he was used to.

He dropped his arms and the warm body next to him grunted. Nash shot out of bed and flopped to the floor, swearing as his ass hit the hard wood. Stars danced in his vision and he blinked, trying to clear them enough to figure out who was looking down at him from the edge of the mattress.

"What the hell is going on with you? Do you usually wake up so squirrely?"

"Cullen?"

Cullen's low chuckle danced over Nash's body like the warmest rush of water. "Yeah, man. Who did you think it was? Or did you just not remember?"

"I tend to take a while to wake up, so if I'm not in my own bed, it freaks me out a little." He hated admitting that, but if he wanted some kind of a longer fling with Cullen, the man had to know some of Nash's quirks. "I'm also not used to having anyone in the bed with me in the morning."

Cullen folded his arms before resting his chin on them. His dark eyes were sparkling with laughter and it looked good on the man. Yet somehow Nash knew it wasn't an emotion Cullen often indulged in.

"I guess I should be glad you didn't attack me."

From where he sat, Nash watched Cullen climb out of bed and stretch. He ran his gaze over the full length of the man standing over him, letting his eyes linger on Cullen's cock. It wasn't as long as Nash's, but it was thicker, and Nash's ass clenched at the memory of it moving inside him. A patch of black hair covered the base of Cullen's shaft. As Nash trailed his gaze over Cullen's body, he smiled.

"You're hairier than most of the guys I've slept with, and bigger too," Nash commented.

"Well, thank you. I'm sorry your flings weren't as endowed as I am." Cullen leaned over, offering Nash a hand.

He took it, marveling at Cullen's strength when he didn't even strain to lift Nash off the floor and onto his feet. He moved right into Cullen's embrace, brushing his lips over Cullen's mouth.

"Hmm…" Cullen hummed, opening to Nash.

After plundering his mouth for a minute or two, Nash eased back, but he didn't let go of Cullen's ass. He grinned and said, "Do we have time for a shower before you take me back to Fallen Creek?"

Cullen glanced over his shoulder at the alarm clock next to the bed and frowned. "Well, you have time for a shower, but if I join you, we won't have time for anything except another nap. I have things I need to do before tonight."

If he'd been that kind of man, he'd pout, but he decided it wasn't fair to try to get Cullen to join him. Not when Cullen was probably going to be fighting for his life later on that night.

"It's your loss then." He gave Cullen's ass a squeeze before stepping farther away. "I'll grab a shower and you can get the coffee going."

"Sounds like a good idea."

Cullen grabbed some sweats from a dresser and tossed them at Nash. He caught them while biting back a moan of protest as Cullen pulled on a pair of jeans and a T-shirt. His phone started ringing and he looked around for his jeans.

"They're on the chair over there." Cullen gestured to a chair in the corner before he left the room.

Nash tugged his phone out and opened it. "Hey there, Ten, what's up?"

"I'm not sure. I think Union might know you've left and where you're heading."

He almost dropped the phone but caught it before it hit the floor. After putting it back up to his ear, he said, "Are you fucking kidding me?"

Ten sighed. "I wish I was, man, but he's acting really weird and is talking about getting some of the guys to go on a road trip."

"Shit." He sat and braced his elbows on his knees, staring at the floor. That wasn't good news. Nash had hoped he'd gotten out of Nashville without anyone knowing where he was headed. "How did he find out?"

"I don't know, but he has hands in a lot of pots. If you used a credit card, or if he had someone run your name, he could've gotten it that way." Ten sounded afraid. "He has friends in the police department as well, Nash. You know that."

"Fuck me," Nash swore.

It wasn't like he'd forgotten all the people Union had blackmailed, but he had thought certain people would have buried his leaving town. Ten wouldn't have said a word about Nash, plus he didn't know where Nash was.

"Thanks for the warning, Ten. I think I know how Union could've found out where I might be. Just keep your head down and don't get in trouble with the club. Call me if you need help. I might be able to get someone to you."

"Don't worry about me, bro. I can take care of myself. Just keep yourself safe. I don't want to lose you." Ten hung up before Nash could say anything else.

Nash stood before making his way into the bathroom. He shut the door, locking it before turning on the fan. He dialed the number he'd hoped he'd never have to use.

"How bad is it?" The gruff voice on the other end didn't bother with pleasantries.

"I'm not sure. Union's telling his guys to get ready for a ride. Ten couldn't tell me any more than that." Nash stared at his reflection in the mirror.

"Of course he couldn't. Union wouldn't risk letting his nephew know anything, especially if it has to do with you. He isn't stupid, he knows Ten will tell you anything." The man on the other end of the connection was quiet for a moment. Then he asked, "Are you safe where you are?"

"For right now, but I don't want to hang around too much longer. The sheriff did a background check on me when I got into town. That must have been how Union figured out where I was." Nash shoved his hand through his hair.

"Damn it, Rhodes. You were supposed to stay under the radar until we got things squared away. You had to run to the cops the first chance you got."

"Shut up. I didn't run to the cops. He was hassling me and it was easier to just let him check me out than argue with him."

"Well, hopefully we can solve the problem before they head out of town. Don't call me again unless Union is standing in front of you or you're dying."

The man hung up and Nash fought the urge to throw his phone against the wall. None of it was his fault. He was following orders, and that meant leaving his old life behind and trying to find a new one.

"Are you taking a shower any time soon?"

He jumped when Cullen's voice came through the bathroom door.

"Yeah, sorry."

Nash took a quick shower then threw on the T-shirt and sweats Cullen had given him. There were socks and a pair of tennis shoes on the bed when he went into the other room.

After finishing, he followed the smell of bacon down the hallway into the kitchen. Cullen looked up and smiled when Nash entered.

Gesturing with his chin, Cullen said, "You can get some coffee over there. I have orange juice and milk as well. Breakfast will be ready in a minute."

"What are you going to do today? Anything special to get ready for your fight with Robinson tonight?"

Cullen set a plate full of eggs, bacon and potatoes in front of him before taking his own seat. "I have to ride the fence, checking to make sure there aren't any posts down. I'll spend the time on my own, getting settled."

"Like meditating?"

"Yes. I don't challenge people to fights very often, so it's best if I spend the time alone, working out my strategy." Cullen started eating.

"Good idea. I'll probably help Jeanette clean up the mess Robinson and his gang left."

Nash ate quickly, suddenly wanting to head back to Fallen Creek. He wanted to check on Jeanette and make sure she was okay. Thinking of Jeanette made him think of the sheriff.

"Have you heard anything about Carter?"

"Actually, I called the sheriff's office while you were taking a shower. He's going to be in the hospital for a while, but there wasn't any permanent damage."

After they'd finished eating, they cleaned their plates and straightened up the kitchen before Cullen grabbed his keys and hat.

"I'll take you back into town."

Nash didn't say anything as they climbed into Cullen's truck and headed back to Fallen Creek. He wanted to ask if he'd get to see Cullen after whatever he and Robinson were doing, but he didn't want to sound clingy or possessive. It wasn't like they were having a relationship or anything. It had been a night of fucking. That was it. Neither of them had declared their undying love.

Of course, it didn't stop him from saying, "I want to come to the fight. I still don't understand why you don't just call the cops on his ass. It certainly seems like everyone knows how Robinson is making his money."

Cullen frowned. "I wish it was that simple. The situation isn't as clear-cut as that, Nash. There are other reasons why I can't just turn him in to the authorities."

As much as Nash wanted to argue, he actually understood what Cullen was talking about. Even though Cullen wasn't part of the gang, he had to think about the risks he was running by saying something to anyone outside of the town. It seemed to be a lot like what Nash had dealt with in the club. Once a man was part of the club, he kept its secrets from everyone on the outside. The club took care of its own problems internally. No involving anyone who could damage the club in some way, and especially no police or law enforcement.

"I get it. It's just like me with the club. We're taught from the moment we ask to join the club that we're to keep quiet and not to let anyone in our business." Nash reached over and rested his hand on Cullen's thigh. "I still want to be there tonight. I get the feeling you might not have any kind of backup, and Robinson will have all his guys."

Cullen covered his hand and squeezed it. "I can't let you come. You're still healing from whatever happened to you in Nashville, plus the attack last night didn't help, I'm sure. You can't help me with this. I'll come to your place afterward and you can see that I'm still alive."

"Are you so confident you'll win?"

Nodding, Cullen turned into the parking lot for The Watering Hole. There were several cars already there, and people coming and going from the bar.

"Yes, I am. Trust me when I say this challenge has been coming for a long time. I just put it off because it didn't mean as much to me before."

"What changed your mind?"

Cullen parked the truck and turned to look at Nash. Before Nash could move, Cullen grabbed for his hand again. For a moment, Nash thought Cullen would kiss him, but the man wasn't that stupid.

"I protect what's mine."

He blinked at the serious tone of Cullen's statement. Who was he laying claim to? Was it Jeanette or him? Could it be both of them?

"Okay." He edged closer to the door.

"Jeanette is my friend and Robinson tried to destroy her business. You made Robinson back down, which no one besides me has ever done. You're on his list to teach a lesson." Cullen squeezed his hand. "I won't let that happen, and if I have to fight Robinson to stop him, I will."

"I can take care of myself," Nash reminded him.

"I know, but Robinson isn't your usual bad guy and his pack isn't one you can deal with on your own. Trust me. I've dealt with people like them most of my life."

Cullen looked serious and Nash wanted to ask him what he meant by that. Before he could say anything, a knock came on the window. Nash jumped, but Cullen acted like he knew the person had been approaching.

Turning, Nash saw Jeanette standing outside the truck. He opened the door and stepped out. Jeanette wrapped her arms around him and hugged him tight.

"I was worried when you disappeared like that last night. Where did you go?" She shot Cullen a quick glance. "I know where you ended up."

"I went to find Cullen. I knew he was going to face Robinson and I wasn't going to let him do it without backup." Nash could feel his face heat up. "Cullen had been attacked, and I didn't want him to be alone last night. Just in case he was hurt worse than we thought."

"Of course." Jeanette winked at him.

Shit! How had she guessed about him and Cullen? Of course, showing up in Cullen's clothes and blushing when he talked about staying the night at Cullen's place probably gave her a clue. Yet she didn't seem very upset with the situation.

Jeanette leaned closer to him. "I don't care what you guys

were up to last night, Nash. It isn't any of my business what goes on between adults. Plus, I've seen a lot in my years, and two guys loving each other isn't going to shock me at all."

"Thank you," he whispered.

Nodding, she smiled at him before turning to look at Cullen. "So are you going to stick around and help clean my place up?"

Cullen shook his head. "Sorry. I have to get back to my place. I'm riding fence today."

"I heard you have a challenge later on." Jeanette crossed her arms and glared at Cullen. "It's about damn time. I've been waiting for you to get off your lazy ass and do something about Robinson for a while now."

"Sorry to have kept ya waiting," Cullen said, a slight hint of an accent to his words now. It was the first time Nash had heard anything that might tell him where Cullen was from.

"It's all right. You're rectifying the situation." She patted his arm.

Nash couldn't believe how patronizing Jeanette sounded. Cullen studied her closely and there was an intriguing gleam in his eyes. It was like the man was trying to figure out something about Jeanette but hadn't quite gotten there yet.

"I have a feeling you could've ended it any time you wanted to, Jeanette, but you chose not to because why? You wanted to teach me a lesson or something?"

She shrugged before turning to walk away. She said over her shoulder, "I'll see you tomorrow after the challenge and we can talk more about it."

Nash had no idea what was going on, but he did know he had to go change his clothes before he helped with the clean-up. He glanced over at Cullen.

"If I promise not to come to the challenge, do you promise to stop by afterward, so I can make sure you're all right?"

Cullen pursed his lips and seemed to think about it before

he nodded. "I'll come and get you when it's over."

As much as Nash wanted to kiss Cullen, he knew better than to do it in the parking lot. He held out his hand for Cullen to shake.

"I'll see you later."

"Yes."

He stood there and watched Cullen climb into his truck and drive away. Nash hated the way he felt as the truck disappeared around the corner. The only other person he'd ever cared about was Ten, and he'd never felt like this around his friend. God, he wanted to run after Cullen, yelling for him not to sacrifice himself to the gang.

Nash wanted to break his promise and go to the challenge. He hated the idea of Cullen going into it without someone watching his back. Nash didn't know if Cullen had any friends in Fallen Creek.

Turning toward the bar, he ran his hands through his hair. Time to go and change before he went to help Jeanette and the others.

* * * *

Nash sat up in his bed, staring around and trying to figure out what had woken him. His body protested every move as he climbed out from under the blankets before heading toward the door of his trailer. Another knock came when he reached his quasi-living room.

He paused before he opened the door. What if it wasn't Cullen like he assumed? What if it was someone sent by Union to take him out? Where had he hidden his gun?

There was no way he could leave it lying out where people could see it, since he didn't want to answer any questions about why he had one. He took a deep breath and practically jumped out of his skin when Cullen's voice came through the door.

"I know you're standing right next to the door, Nash. Open up and let me in. I don't want anyone seeing me here this late at night."

"How did you know I was there?" he asked as he opened the door.

Cullen pushed in, shutting the door quickly behind him. Nash winced when he saw his face. Wounds marred most of it. Nash started to reach and touch Cullen's cheek, but Cullen moved away.

"Why don't you pack a bag and come out to my place for the night?" Cullen sat at the small Formica table in the kitchen section of Nash's trailer. The slow way Cullen moved told Nash he was hurting.

"Why aren't you on your way to the hospital? I assume you won, since you're here."

He stalked back to his bedroom and began to toss clothes into his duffle bag. After opening his nightstand drawer, he realized he'd stuffed the pistol there so it would be close to him during the night. For some reason, he stuck the gun into his bag. It wasn't like he didn't trust Cullen, but his instincts were saying Union was coming and it would be his life if he wasn't ready for the man.

"Yes, I did win, and there are several reasons why I can't go to the hospital. They'll want to know how I got my injuries, then they'll want to know about Robinson. I can't tell them I killed the bastard." Cullen's voice drifted from the kitchen.

A soft grunt followed, and Nash decided he had everything he needed. It wasn't like he was going to be wearing pajamas to bed or anything. He picked up the duffle and slung it over his shoulder with his own grunt. After stopping in the bathroom, he grabbed his pain pills and tucked them into an outside pocket on the bag.

"Let's go. We need to get to your place, so I can take a look at your wounds."

He gestured to the entrance and restrained the need to help Cullen to his feet. They slowly walked down the steps and over to Cullen's truck. Nash opened the passenger door and tossed his bag behind the seat before turning to hold out his hand.

"I'll drive to your place."

Cullen looked like he wanted to say no, but Nash wasn't going to let him drive.

"Man, you look like shit, and I'm pretty sure you feel like it as well. Letting me drive doesn't make you weak or a pussy. It makes you smart. I don't want you passing out behind the wheel and killing us both." He wiggled his fingers in front of Cullen's face.

Cullen growled slightly but tossed Nash the keys. He caught them and watched Cullen climb into the cab. Again, he respected Cullen's need to prove his strength and kept his hands to himself.

After climbing inside, but before he turned the truck on, he slid his hand around the back of Cullen's head to draw the man to him. He gently pressed his lips to Cullen's mouth. Their kiss didn't getter hotter or deeper, but it helped settle Nash's nerves.

He'd seen more men than he could count beaten up and injured, and their pain had never affected him the way Cullen's did. He'd spent most of the day and night imagining all the bad things that could have happened to Cullen during the fight.

They eased apart and Cullen rested his head against the back of the seat.

"Just take me home, Nash. I'll let you fuss over me when we get there, but I'm not going to the hospital."

"All right." He turned the truck on and drove out of the parking lot. "You killed Robinson? How did his gang like that?"

"They'll deal with it. Those who don't like it can either challenge me or they can leave. They're going to have to find new ways of making a living because there won't be any more drugs being made or sold." Cullen's eyes were closed.

"What did you do with the body?"

Cullen peered at him for a second before shutting his eyes

again. "His body isn't my concern. The pack will take care of it. More than likely, they'll either burn or bury him. As long as he's gone and I'm in charge, I don't fucking care what happens to it."

They stopped at a red light and Nash glanced over at Cullen. He frowned and looked closer. Cullen's face didn't appear as cut up as Nash had originally thought. The wounds weren't bleeding as much, and actually some of the injuries seemed like they were healing.

Cullen opened his eyes and their gazes connected. There was a gleam of red in Cullen's irises that caused a shiver to run down Nash's spine.

"What are you?"

Cullen blinked and the red went away, but a short look of surprise crossed the man's face. "What are you talking about?" Cullen cleared his throat and winced. "Did you get the bar cleaned up?"

"Yeah, though Jeanette will have to order a full shipment of liquor before she can open. Robinson's gang did a number on the alcohol."

Chapter Eight

Cullen gritted his teeth as he climbed out of the truck. He'd managed to deflect Nash's question by getting the man to talk about the clean-up at The Watering Hole. What had Nash seen in his eyes to make him ask that question?

Christ! He hurt in every atom of his body, and he'd never felt that way before. Maybe that was why he'd never challenged anyone — because, subconsciously, he knew how painful the whole fucking thing would be.

By the morning, his wounds would be pretty much healed, especially if he could sneak out and shift. In his wolf form, his injuries tended to get better quicker.

He leaned against the post of his porch while Nash unlocked the front door. Cullen started stripping the minute they stepped inside. He left a trail of clothes down the hallway into his bathroom.

"I'm going out and grabbing my bag. I'll be back in here to look at your wounds in a minute. Don't get in the shower until I'm sure you don't need stitches or something," Nash said from where he stood near the door.

"If I do, are you going to perform the surgery?"

Cullen studied his reflection in the mirror over the sink. If he'd had any serious wounds, they had started to heal while he'd gone to get Nash. He'd declined any kind of medical care from Robinson's old pack. It wasn't because he thought they would try to kill him — they were all followers. Not one of them was going to challenge him for Alpha of the pack. But none of them knew what to do with a needle if it didn't involve injecting some kind of drug into their veins. He didn't trust them to patch him up either.

"Jesus Christ!"

He met Nash's shocked gaze in the mirror. Cullen could only imagine what his back looked like. Not as bad as his stomach, though. Robinson had gotten in several slashes with his hind legs during their fight.

"It looks like you got mauled by a wolf. Did Robinson have more of those animals around?"

Nash laid his hand on Cullen's back and Cullen shuddered at his touch. His body was absorbing the pain while healing and exhaustion washed over him. He let his head drop forward, giving Nash a better look at his body.

"No. It wasn't the dogs, but I'm not in any condition to explain at the moment."

"Hush. It's all right. I'll be quick and then you can take a shower. Do you want something to eat before you go to bed?"

Cullen nodded. His wolf needed to eat because of the energy he'd expended during the fight. "I have a couple of steaks in the fridge. If you want, you can heat them up slightly. I like my meat rare."

"Okay."

He allowed Nash to turn him enough for the light to hit his back. Nash's soft hiss told Cullen that his wounds hadn't healed as quickly as he thought. It was because he needed to shift and let whatever kind of magic that was inside him heal the rest of them.

"Fuck, Cullen, I haven't seen anyone as roughed up as you are, and I've seen plenty of 'lessons' taught to people the club didn't like."

"Now you know one reason why it took me so long to challenge Robinson. I knew this was going to happen." Cullen sucked in a deep breath as Nash pressed a kiss to one piece of his bruised skin.

Nash grabbed a washcloth and got it wet with warm water. Cullen gripped the edge of the counter while Nash began to wash the blood and dirt off.

He stayed silent and let Nash take care of him for the next

thirty minutes. When the last inch of his flesh was clean, Cullen grinned slightly at Nash, who had moved to stand in front of him.

"Do I need stitches?"

Nash frowned, staring at his chest where some of the deepest slashes were. "No. Now that the blood is off, it looks like you weren't hurt as badly as I thought you were. Why don't you take a shower to get the rest of the dirt off? I'll make you some steaks and we'll bandage a couple of the deeper wounds before you head to bed."

"Thank you."

It was going to be hard to hold onto the wolf while he slept, but he couldn't risk Nash discovering him. So he would have to pretend to rest, and once Nash fell asleep, he'd sneak off behind the barn to shift. He'd set up a small nest of blankets in a lean-to far enough from the paddocks and barns so as not to bother his horses with his comings and goings.

By the time he'd finished washing up and went out to his kitchen, Nash was plating up the steaks.

"Here you go."

"Thanks."

After sitting, he picked up the knife and fork, taking bite after bite without pause. His wolf was ravenous and he wanted to rest so badly. He managed not to lick the plate clean, but it was close.

"I think you're done."

Nash grabbed the plate from him and he growled. He took control of his wolf, pushing it back in his mind, so it wouldn't do anything like that again.

"Sorry. Guess I'm still a little pumped up from the fight. I'm just going to head to bed. Are you coming with me?"

"Yeah. Let me clean up first."

Cullen stood and took Nash's hand in his. He tugged Nash closer to him, lowering his head to bring their lips together. His lover moaned into his mouth, which allowed Cullen to sweep his tongue in. He tasted the beer Nash had drunk while Cullen had eaten.

His wolf loved the way Nash melted into his embrace. How Nash accepted Cullen's dominance over him and didn't fight what Cullen wanted. While Cullen would have loved to bend Nash over the kitchen table, he wasn't up to fucking.

After easing away, he smiled slightly. "I'd love to fuck you right now, but I'm just not up to it at the moment."

Nash chuckled. "I got it, man. We can get busy after you recover from the fight."

"Certainly. Leave the dishes. I can get them tomorrow morning."

"All right."

Cullen liked the fact that Nash didn't argue with him about cleaning up. They walked hand-in-hand down the hallway to Cullen's bedroom. After stripping silently, they climbed under the covers and curled up in each other's arms. He knew his wolf would wake him up in the early hours of the morning so he could go and shift.

He woke shortly after moonrise and slid out from under Nash's arms. Cullen stood next to the bed, not wanting to leave until he was sure Nash wasn't going to wake up. When his lover showed no signs of knowing he'd left, Cullen headed outside.

His horses hung their heads over the tops of their stall doors, watching as he strolled through to the back of the barn. He'd built the lean-to for the nights when the wolf was so strong it took control of him and he spent most of his time in his beast's form.

Once he was out of sight of the house, he paused and allowed his inner beast to take over. Usually there was some pain as his bones and flesh re-created themselves into the form of a wolf. When the transformation finished, Cullen shook himself, rejoicing in the feel of his four legs and the thick coat he wore.

He took off down the trail toward the hills behind his place. His wounds still ached and twinged once in a while as he stretched his muscles, yet he could almost feel the rest of his injuries healing, even while he ran.

Cullen traveled over half of his land before he turned around to head home. After reaching the lean-to, he shifted back and cleaned up with the hose and a cloth he'd left there. The thought of curling up next to Nash in his warm bed drove Cullen to rush back inside.

Nash was lying in the middle of the bed when Cullen returned to the bedroom. After slipping back under the covers, he wrapped his arms around Nash and tugged him close.

"Where did you go?" Nash mumbled.

"Just had to take a piss," Cullen said.

"Hmm…seemed like you were gone longer than that," Nash commented.

Cullen wasn't sure what to say, so he winged it. "I thought I heard something outside when I headed to the bathroom, so I went out to the barn to check on the horses."

Nash grunted but didn't say anything else. Cullen smoothed his hand up and down Nash's arm and buried his face in the curls at Nash's nape. He felt the steady rise and fall of Nash's chest as the man breathed. The easy rhythm caused Cullen to fall asleep. His wolf and man, for the first time, were content to be with another.

* * * *

Cullen jerked awake when the body in his arms disappeared. After sitting up, he blinked at the gorgeous ass walking away from him. Without thinking, he whistled low, causing Nash to pause and glance over his shoulder at him.

"Well, thank you." Nash winked and continued out of the room.

Cullen leaned back against the headboard, tucking the blankets around his hips. He looked down to check the wounds on his chest. There were several pink scars that looked months old. He poked at one of them, wincing a little at the hint of pain. It was more like a bruise than a deep injury.

He heard the toilet flush and the water run as Nash washed up. Cullen was glad the lights weren't on when Nash strolled back into the room. He didn't know how he was going to explain how well his wounds were doing. Nash wasn't going to accept the answer that they weren't as bad as he'd thought when Cullen had picked him up. The man wasn't stupid and Cullen hadn't thought up a good reason yet.

Nash climbed into bed, but instead of snuggling up to Cullen, he pushed the blankets down and ran his hand over Cullen's stomach to his groin. He moaned as Nash cupped his cock with his wide hand.

"I thought you might like a little help taking your mind off your injuries," Nash commented. Grinning, he tightened his grip a little more and tugged slightly.

"Fuck." Cullen growled as his shaft stiffened.

Maybe if he were really human, he would be interested in fucking, but his body still wouldn't be able to do it. Thank God he was a shifter. He was more than up for the challenge.

"Harder," he ordered, and lust shot through him as Nash obeyed.

The mere fact that Nash was willing to submit excited Cullen more than any other lover had. Of course, Cullen hadn't found a man more suited to his wants and desires than Nash.

Nash started to stroke his hand up and down, pumping Cullen's cock. Cullen liked the friction of Nash's rough skin over his smooth length.

He rested his hand on Nash's shoulder, trailing his fingers over the man, learning the dips and swells of muscles along Nash's back. Using light pressure, he gently urged Nash to ease over between his legs.

"Put your mouth on me," Cullen demanded.

There was no hesitation from Nash at the order. Nash wrapped his full lips around the flared head of Cullen's cock, drawing a moan from Cullen. The suction of Nash's mouth was driving Cullen crazy and he cupped the back of Nash's head. With easy pressure, he encouraged Nash to take more of his length with each bob of his head.

Cullen groaned when his cock hit the back of Nash's throat and the man swallowed around it. "Fuck me."

Nash grunted, and Cullen glanced down to see Nash humping the bed. He tapped Nash's shoulder and when he looked up at him, Cullen grinned.

"Why don't you swing around and I'll take care of that for you?"

Nash let Cullen slip out of his mouth. "Are you sure?"

"No point in letting you take care of yourself when I'm perfectly capable of helping you." He winked.

He swore he smelled smoke from the speed Nash moved. In seconds, Nash knelt over him and his erection brushed Cullen's lips. He opened and took as much of Nash in as he could.

"Oh, holy fuck, I love your mouth."

Cullen scraped his teeth over the velvety flesh of Nash's cock, hoping he reminded the guy to show some love to him. Nash chuckled and took his cock back in.

They rocked together, matching suction and swirl of tongues. Each swipe of Nash's over Cullen's head drove him closer and closer to the edge. He hoped he was doing the same to Nash. A thought hit him and he slipped his finger into his mouth alongside Nash's cock.

When he'd gotten it as wet as he could, he removed it and rubbed the tip over Nash's pucker. The feeling of Nash's groan around his shaft made Cullen shudder and he breached Nash's ass slowly but inexorably, until he was in as far as he could be.

He twisted slightly and Nash tightened his muscles around Cullen's finger and jerked. *Guess I hit the right spot,* Cullen thought, as Nash shuddered each time Cullen hit his gland.

Soon they lost all rhythm, shoving and grunting until Cullen's climax overtook him. He yanked his mouth off Nash and shouted as his cum spilled from him. When Nash sucked the last drop from him, he flipped his lover over onto his back and returned the favor.

Nash grabbed hold of Cullen's head and held him still while he fucked his mouth. His wolf fought the hold for a second, but Cullen suppressed the beast, letting Nash control the depth of his thrusts.

"I'm gonna come," Nash warned him.

Cullen tapped Nash's hip, letting the man know it was okay to let go. With a shout, Nash came, flooding Cullen's mouth to the point where his cum dripped from the edges of his lips. He swallowed as much as he could and cleaned Nash when he was done shaking.

He rolled off to the side, breathing heavily, while Nash pushed up on his elbow, leaned over and licked his cum from Cullen's face. He dropped back down to rest his head on Cullen's chest.

"Thank you," Nash whispered.

Staring at the ceiling, Cullen frowned. "Thanks for what? I didn't do anything except blow you."

Nash blew out a puff of air and Cullen realized he didn't really want to explain what he'd meant by his statement. He pushed Nash over so he could look down at him.

"Just tell me, man. I won't think badly of you. I'm not a mind reader." Cullen nuzzled Nash's jaw, and his wolf growled in his mind at the scent of sweat on Nash's skin.

Nash shrugged. "I guess I'm just thanking you for caring about me enough to check up on me."

"Hey, you're the first person in a long time who I've cared enough for to worry about." Cullen trailed his fingers over Nash's cheek. "It's weird how quickly I've become attached to you. Probably not such a good thing because you're leaving soon."

Cullen watched Nash bite his bottom lip and wondered

what Nash wasn't saying. He didn't think the man really wanted to stay here because, really, who would? Fallen Creek was in the foothills of the Rocky Mountains and it was quite a drive to get from the town to any kind of big city. A guy like Nash, who was used to the hustle and bustle of a city like Nashville, wouldn't enjoy the slower pace of Fallen Creek.

He snorted silently to himself. Hell, there were times when he didn't like the small-town feel. The townspeople could be a nosy lot at the best of times, and hiding his wolf had been difficult as well, especially during the full moon.

The alarm went off and he laughed. "I have to get up and feed the animals."

"I'll make breakfast while you do that, then you can take me back into town."

Cullen eased out of bed and tugged on some jeans. Before he could put on a shirt, Nash sat up and turned on the lamp next to the bed. Cullen couldn't get his T-shirt on fast enough.

"What the fuck?"

He tensed when Nash jumped up and grabbed his shoulder. Cullen didn't fight Nash's insistent pulling. He knew what Nash was reacting to, so he held his arms out from his sides and let the man study him.

"Where the hell are all your wounds?"

"Maybe I wasn't as injured as we thought last night." It was the only thing he could think of to say.

"I wasn't that tired or drunk, Cullen. I know exactly how bad your wounds were." Nash poked his side, and Cullen winced as Nash's finger hit a bruise. "Now it looks like your fight was a month or two ago, and you've just got a few bruises and scars."

Looking down, Cullen saw the long, pink scars of freshly healed wounds. "I'm a fast healer?"

"Are you asking me or what?" Nash shook his head. "We're going to get dressed and then you're going to tell me the truth. I know there's something else going on here."

Cullen closed his eyes and nodded. *Christ!* He had to come up with something better than what he'd already said, or he was just going to have to tell the truth about being a shifter. Neither option was one he wanted to think about.

They got dressed in silence, then went out to the kitchen where the coffee pot had already been brewing. Cullen poured himself a mug before getting another one down for Nash. After doctoring his coffee the way he liked, Cullen sat at the table and watched as Nash got his ready.

"Tell me the truth, Cullen. Where are your wounds? You should still be in bed from them."

"I'm not sure what I should tell you." Cullen rubbed the back of his neck. "Whatever I say, you won't believe me."

"Try me."

Cullen stared into Nash's eyes, and there was a certain light in them that made him think maybe Nash would understand what Cullen told him. Maybe Nash would accept the fact that Cullen was a shifter. Then Nash blinked and the look was gone.

Staring at his coffee, Cullen took a deep breath, trying to figure out what he was going to say. His phone rang before he could come up with a reasonable lie. Relief shot through him as he stood then headed back to his bedroom where his phone was.

"Hello?"

"Hey, Cullen, this is Deputy Barker. I'm calling because Sheriff Carter would like to talk to you."

Cullen frowned. "I thought the sheriff would be too injured to talk to anyone."

"The doctors think he should rest, but he's insisting he needs to talk to you first." Barker sounded annoyed.

"Fine. I'll be right there." He ended the call.

He turned to find Nash standing in the doorway, arms folded and eyebrows raised.

"Sheriff Carter wants to talk to me."

"Hmm…very convenient. If I didn't know better, I'd think he called so you wouldn't have to talk to me."

Cullen chuckled. "I don't have that kind of power. I assume Carter wants to talk to me about Robinson and the challenge."

"Probably. Take a shower and I'll cook breakfast. After you eat and feed your animals, you can drive me back to the bar before you stop by the hospital." Nash swung around before heading back toward the kitchen.

Cullen did as his lover suggested. Once he was clean and dressed, he joined Nash in the kitchen, where they quickly ate. Nash didn't seem inclined to chat anymore and Cullen needed to make sure his animals had food.

"I'll clean up in here while you go out to the barn. When you're done, we'll head back to town." Nash paused for a moment. "But don't think this talk is over. You're still going to answer my questions."

He nodded, not knowing what to say. After putting on his boots and hat, he strolled outside, making his way to the barn. He fed the horses, then watered them. When he knew they had cleaned their buckets, he let each of them out in the corral, with some flakes of hay scattered about for them. They'd be fine while he was away.

Finally, he couldn't think of anything else to do, so he went back inside. Nash was sitting in the living room, reading one of Cullen's books. He looked up as Cullen stopped in the archway.

"Why don't you have a TV?"

Cullen shrugged. "I never saw the importance of having one. I watch shows on my computer sometimes, but I mostly like to read."

Nash pursed his lips but didn't say anything else about it. "Let's go. You need to get to the hospital, and I need to get home."

They gathered their things before heading out to Cullen's truck. The ride back to town was silent as well. It was almost like Nash had decided to keep his questions to himself for the moment. Cullen appreciated it because he really didn't want to talk about his wolf, or anything else for that matter.

After dropping Nash at the bar and promising to call him later, Cullen drove into the next town to get to the hospital. He got to Carter's room just as a doctor was leaving it.

"I hope you're O'Murphy. The sheriff needs to rest if he's to heal, and he's giving me a hard time because he wants to talk to you." The doctor studied him.

"Yes, ma'am. I'm Cullen O'Murphy. I'll only take up a few minutes of the sheriff's time, then he can go to sleep like a good boy."

She huffed in annoyance. "I doubt that man has ever been a good boy."

Cullen laughed. "You're probably right."

He walked in the room, finding Carter sitting up in his bed and staring at the door.

"I've been waiting for you to get here."

"Sorry. Had a few things to take care of before I could come." Cullen propped his hands on his hips. "What did you want to talk to me about?"

"Did you kill him?"

He didn't have to ask who the sheriff was talking about.

"Yes, I did. The challenge was last night and I killed him. There will be no more drugs coming from Fallen Creek or my pack. I will ensure that with deadly force, if necessary." Cullen snarled, baring his teeth. "It's time the pack learns how a real Alpha runs things."

"What about the body?" Carter grimaced. "I'm not going to find him somewhere and have to do an investigation, am I?"

Cullen shook his head. "No. I left it with the pack and told them they had to deal with it. I'm meeting with Robinson's Betas today to see what they did and discuss the new rules with them."

He sat in the chair next to Carter's bed and stared at the sheriff. Carter was covered in bruises and bandages, causing Cullen to wince.

"They did a number on you," he commented.

The sheriff nodded. "Yeah. Thanks for helping me out

with that as well."

"No problem. Couldn't let Robinson kill you. It would bring down too much attention on the town." He grinned at the grunt Carter gave him. "And I kind of like you. Don't want to have to deal with another sheriff if something happened to you."

"Thanks."

Cullen waved away Carter's gratitude. "It needed to be done. Now I have to get back to my ranch. Have to check the rest of the herd before I call a pack meeting."

"Don't you want to know how I know about you and the others?"

"I'll catch up with you later about that. You need to rest, so you aren't going anywhere." Cullen stood before leaning over and touching Carter's knee. "Besides, I know you won't say anything to anyone about us. I mean, you haven't let on until now that you knew. Also, you know what I'm capable of, and while I don't want any attention from the outside, I'll deal with any threat."

Carter nodded, his expression showing that he'd gotten the warning in Cullen's words. Cullen left and headed back to his truck. He had to check on his cattle then figure out what he was going to say to the pack.

Chapter Nine

"How's Cullen this morning?"

Nash glanced up from where he crouched, painting a chair. Jeanette stood over him, arms folded and her eyes gleaming with curiosity.

"Surprisingly, he's fine." He frowned.

"Why do you say it that way?" Jeanette gestured for him to put the paintbrush down and follow her. "I had Marley from the diner bring us over some lunch. It's time to eat and I want to hear about the challenge last night."

He groaned as he straightened. He'd been so worried about Cullen's injuries that he'd never given his own a thought. His body still ached from the old wounds and all the new bruises hadn't helped either. Nash placed his hands at the small of his back and stretched, trying to get the kinks out.

"You didn't have to buy me lunch," he told Jeanette when he joined her at the bar.

She wrinkled her nose at him. "Yes, I did. You've only been here a few days, and already you've been beat up because of me. You had to help rebuild my bar, plus get it ready for customers. That's a lot to ask of a man who's only passing through."

After sitting, he shrugged, pulling the Styrofoam container toward him. "It's no big deal. I'm here, and my momma would tan my hide if she found out I didn't help you when you needed it."

"I know I'd like your mother if I ever met her." Jeanette sat next to him before opening her dinner. Instead of taking a bite, she poked him with her fork. "So talk."

"Cullen showed up at my place after the fight. He was really beat to shit, with gaping wounds on his stomach and back. Almost looked like he'd been mauled by a dog or something."

Nash shot Jeanette a glance when she snorted, but she waved for him to continue.

"I wanted to take him to the hospital, but he said he'd be fine and just to take him home. We went back to the ranch, where I cleaned him up, and we went to sleep." Nash stabbed at his salad.

Jeanette stayed silent, and he figured it was so she wouldn't distract Nash. He considered not going on, because he didn't really want to talk about Cullen's miraculous healing before he discussed it with his lover.

"I'm sure you did more than sleep, but I don't want to know the details." She winked then waved her hand again. "Go on."

He sighed, somehow knowing Jeanette wouldn't give up until he'd told her the whole truth.

"When we got up this morning, all of Cullen's injuries were healed. They looked like he'd gotten them months ago. I hadn't been drinking or anything like that. I know exactly how they looked last night."

"What did Cullen have to say about it?"

Nash laughed and rolled his eyes. "First, he tried to tell me his wounds weren't as bad as I thought they were. When I called him out on it, he told me he was a fast healer. Now, he might be telling the truth, but no one heals as fast as he did."

"True. I assume you called him on that bullshit as well," she asked.

"Yes, ma'am. I was going to make him tell me the truth, but the sheriff called and wanted to talk to him. He dropped me off before heading to the hospital. I did tell him we were going to talk when we saw each other again."

They finished their food at the same time and she cleaned up their containers. He watched as she went behind the bar to pour them both a shot of whiskey. Nash took the glass she shoved toward him.

"Isn't it a little early in the day to be drinking? Unless you have a problem." Even though he asked, he swigged it back and hissed as the liquor burned on the way down.

"Honey, I think you're going to want a drink when Cullen gets around to telling you the truth."

Nash let the glass drop from his hand and glared at Jeanette. "What the hell? Do you know what he's going to tell me?"

"Yes."

"How the fuck do you know? Do you know what is going on in this town?"

Jeanette drank her shot instead of looking at him. "I've been here a long time, Nash. I know where all the skeletons are buried in this town and I know the people who live here better than they know themselves."

He studied her for a moment and worry began to rise in his chest. If she knew all that, then what had she figured out about him? He didn't need anyone knowing about him.

Before he could ask her, the door opened, and they both turned to see Cullen walking into the bar. Nash hadn't realized it had been that long since Cullen had dropped him off.

"Hello. I was passing by and thought I'd drop in to see if you need anything." Cullen stalked across the floor to grip Nash's shoulder.

"We're fine here. I have to get something from the office." Jeanette patted Cullen's hand then left them alone.

Nash swiveled around on his bar stool to face Cullen. His lover bent down to brush a kiss over his lips.

"What have you and Jeanette been gossiping about?"

He thought about not saying anything but figured Cullen was a big boy. The man could deal with the truth.

"She told me she knows what your explanation of your quick healing was going to be. She was telling me she knows where all the skeletons are hidden in the town."

"Hmm..." Cullen didn't look happy.

"Is she right? Does she know why you healed so fast? What does she know and you won't tell me?"

Cullen shook his head. "I can't go into it right now, Nash. I have to go and meet the pack. I need to kick their asses into gear."

"But you're going to tell me eventually," Nash informed him.

"Yes, I know, but I don't think you'll believe me."

Nash stood, pushing into Cullen's personal space. He slid his hand around to cup the back of Cullen's neck to encourage him to lower his head. They crushed their lips together and dueled with their tongues. While Nash wanted to give in to Cullen's demand and allow him to take over the kiss, he fought that urge. He would be equal this time and not submissive.

Cullen growled as he grasped Nash's hips, yanking him tight against him. Nash softened his grip and his body, leaning into Cullen. He let his head drop to the side and moaned when Cullen trailed kisses along his neck.

The sound of a door closing broke them apart. Nash shook his head to clear the haze of lust fogging his brain. Cullen frowned but didn't move away from him.

"I wasn't trying to change the subject, but I think you should trust me a little more. You might be surprised about what I'll believe or not."

He watched as Cullen shrugged.

The man was an amazing fuck, and he seemed to understand Nash's need to be dominated in a way none of Nash's previous lovers had. Of course, Nash never would have admitted that when he lived in Nashville. It would have been too easy for Union to find out about it, and knowing the club's sergeant-at-arms was secretly submissive would have freaked Union the fuck out.

"Maybe I'll be surprised by how you react." Cullen glanced at his watch. "I need to get going. Have to meet with Robinson's pack and lay down the law."

Nash didn't point out the fact that Cullen had told him that already. He figured the man was a little off his game for some reason.

"Then you'd better head out. I don't want you to miss your meeting. I'll come out to your place tonight when I get done here."

Nodding, Cullen reached into his front pocket to pull out a ring of keys. Nash watched as Cullen took one of those keys off before holding it out to him.

"Here's the key to my front door. If I'm not home when you get there, go on in and make yourself at home."

Before he could get over his shock, Cullen had kissed him and left. Nash stood and stared down at the key in his hand.

"Oh, Cullen's gone, huh? I thought he'd be staying longer. Hell, I had some jobs lined up for him."

Nash jerked in surprise when Jeanette spoke from right beside him. Chuckling, she slapped him on the shoulder.

"Sorry to scare you, honey. I thought you heard me come in."

"That's all right. I was thinking about something else." He started to slide the key into his pocket. "What can I do for you?"

"What's that?" Jeanette snapped her hand out and grabbed the key from Nash. "Is this to Cullen's house? Did he really give you a key to his place?"

"Yes." Nash rubbed the nape of his neck, wishing she didn't sound so intrigued.

"Holy shit! I didn't know it had gotten that serious."

"I don't know that it is. I think the whole Robinson thing might have distracted him. He probably got a few steps outside before he realized what he did."

"Cullen doesn't do anything without thinking about it first. Trust me. He knew exactly what he was doing by giving you this." She held up the key. "You might think it was a spur-of-the-moment kind of thing, but it means more than you can imagine, especially for a man like Cullen."

Nash snatched the key from her then shoved it in his

pocket. "What kind of man is Cullen?"

"A lone wolf, though that's going to change now he's killed Robinson. For a long time, it was just him. His parents died several years ago, but I got the feeling that even when they were alive, he was very much alone." Jeanette sounded sad.

Nash knew what it was like to be alone. While he had his mother and Ten, much of his time was spent on his own. He had to use so much energy to hide who he really was that he didn't have time to make any close friends. Thank God, Ten was willing to stick with him, or Nash really would be alone.

Yet he'd never been as real with anyone as he had been with Cullen. He hadn't told him the entire truth of why he was traveling to Santa Monica. Should he be willing to tell Cullen his truth? It would only be fair, since he wasn't giving any ground on Cullen telling him his secrets.

* * * *

Nash parked his bike at the side of Cullen's porch before climbing off to stretch. His back cracked and he grimaced. Would there ever be a time when he would be able to just lie on the beach, drink some beer and not do a damn thing for a while?

He was tired of hurting and doing shit for other people. One of these days, he wasn't going to answer the phone when someone called him. The whinny of a horse broke his reverie and Nash grabbed his bag from the back of his bike.

After letting himself in to Cullen's house, he dropped the bag in Cullen's bedroom before stripping. He took a quick shower, though he was tempted to stay under the warm water for an hour or so, just to loosen his tight muscles.

He dried off then dressed in sweats and a T-shirt. Nash gathered a load of dirty clothes — his and Cullen's — to toss into the washer. No sense in acting like he was a stranger in Cullen's house. He knew where most of the things he needed were and he didn't have a problem searching until he found the other things.

Once the load was in, he strolled into the kitchen. He struggled for a few moments, trying to figure out how to get Cullen's coffee pot going, but, luckily, he was a smart guy, and he smiled a couple of minutes later when the smell of coffee filled the air.

As he sipped from his cup, Nash wandered into the living room to sit on the couch. The whole place had a rather sterile feel to it. The pictures hanging on the walls were generic and Nash couldn't get a sense of who lived in the house.

Maybe Cullen's presence would be strongest in the bedroom. Nash took his cup back to the kitchen, rinsed and set it in the sink. He stared out of the window, studying the land behind the main building. There were horses in the paddocks, and he could make out the cattle beyond the fences. He didn't know anything about ranching or being a cowboy. He simply knew Cullen looked fucking gorgeous in his faded jeans and cowboy hat.

Nash would have to get Cullen to take him around the ranch. He'd like to see what the land Cullen had chosen to make his home looked like. Returning to the bedroom, Nash sat on the bed, leaning back against the headboard.

He looked around the room and frowned. Nothing, not even generic pictures on the wall. Nash's place back in Nashville had been sparse, but it hadn't been as barren as Cullen's house. Was it because, like Jeanette had said, Cullen had been alone for most of his life and never felt the need to make memories or put down permanent roots? In a way, the thought made Nash sad, and that emotion made him uncomfortable.

Nash heard the door open and called out, "I'm in the bedroom."

A grunt was all he got. After climbing off the bed, he padded down the hall to lean in the doorway of the kitchen. Cullen had the refrigerator door open and was standing there, studying the contents like they held the secret to the universe.

"Are you hungry?" Cullen sounded tired and annoyed. Nash wasn't sure if he was upset with Nash or just life in general.

"Actually, I stopped by the diner on the way here and got dinner for us. We just have to warm it up."

Cullen must have spotted the boxes because he pulled them out then shut the fridge. Nash watched as Cullen got down dishes and glasses. He moved into the room to get the silverware. They got dinner ready then ate in silence, and Nash didn't say anything when Cullen stood and went out of the back door before they could discuss what else had gone on.

It wasn't like Nash was going anywhere. He'd get the truth from the man before the morning came. He rinsed the plates then put them in the dishwasher. Nash grabbed a beer out of the fridge then went to the living room, where he planned on waiting for Cullen to come back inside.

Nash must have dozed off because he jerked awake when the cushion next to him dipped down, causing him to lean to his right. His head landed on a hard shoulder and he grunted.

"Sorry I woke you." Cullen didn't sound sorry.

"No biggie. I was waiting for you anyway." He didn't move, though, snuggling closer, and Cullen lifted his arm to wrap it around him.

"Why were you waiting for me?"

He tilted his head to look up at Cullen and smiled. "You have something to tell me about why your injuries healed so quickly."

Cullen's jaw tightened, as if he was gritting his teeth. After a moment of tense silence, Cullen sighed.

"Fine. I'll tell you, but you aren't going to believe me."

Nash snorted. "You keep saying that, but how do you know what I'll believe and what I won't?"

He toppled flat on the couch as Cullen shot to his feet. Nash lay there for a minute, watching Cullen pace. The man clenched his hands and seemed to be having some kind of internal debate. Nash thought about telling Cullen he didn't have to share any of his secrets.

Rolling over onto his back, Nash stared at the ceiling and argued mentally. What was he thinking? Was it really important to find out Cullen's secrets? It wasn't like he was planning on staying around Fallen Creek much longer, and, once he left, he'd be taking all the walls Cullen had built around his personal life with him as he went.

"Fuck!" Cullen yelled.

Nash looked at him. "What?"

"I just can't think of any plausible lie that could explain what happened to me." Cullen whirled around and glared at him. "Are you worth me baring my soul?"

Was he? There were times when Nash wasn't sure he was worth anything to anyone, not even his mother. Of course, Mom would argue with that thought. She loved him and always said she never regretted anything that had happened since he was born.

What could he say to convince Cullen he was the right guy to spill all of his secrets to?

"I guess, if I were honest, I'd say no. I'm not worth it. Yet I still want to know, and I hope you can come up with a reason to let me into your personal circle."

Cullen snorted. "What personal circle? Man, I don't have any friends or family left."

"What about Jeanette?" Nash thought Cullen and the bar owner were pretty close.

"She's not really a friend, and she certainly isn't family." Cullen shook his head. "My parents are gone, and we moved around so much when I was younger that I never made any friends."

Nash couldn't understand that. He'd lived in Nashville all his life, and Ten was his oldest friend. Never having someone to confide in seemed like it would be lonely.

He watched in surprise as Cullen strolled over and sat on the floor next to the couch. Nash didn't flinch away when Cullen lifted his hand to trail his finger over his nose. He kissed the tip of Cullen's finger as it passed over his lips.

"I'm a…"

Nash's phone rang, interrupting what Cullen was about to say.

"Fuck."

"You can ignore it."

Unfortunately, Nash knew who was calling from the ring tone, and it wasn't someone he could ignore. He shoved to his feet to head to the kitchen, where he'd tossed his phone on the counter when he'd first got in.

He snatched it up before it could stop ringing. Nash answered it. "Nash."

"Bad news." The voice sounded annoyed.

Nash propped his hip against the edge and glared at the floor. "Give it to me."

"By the time our man got to Nashville, Union was gone with two of his top men."

"Shit. What about Ten?"

All Nash could think about was Union killing Ten before he left town. If that happened, Nash would search out Union himself and kill the bastard.

"Don't worry. My man got him out of Nashville without any problem. He's being moved to one of our safe houses."

Relief rushed through Nash and the release of tension caused his shoulders to droop a little. He let his chin hit his chest as he sighed.

"Thanks for that." He was grateful for what they had done for his friend, even though it was their fault Ten was in danger in the first place. "What do I do now?"

The man on the other end cleared his throat. "Well, from what we've figured out, Union has a two-day head start, and he knows where you are. I'm pretty sure he got the information from the police when the sheriff in Fallen Creek sent a request for your file to the Nashville PD."

"Figures the one time I try to be upstanding, it bites me in the ass." Nash shoved his hand through his hair. "What are my orders?"

"Your orders are to stay in Fallen Creek and let Union find you. We know what happened there the other night. So you have to debrief the new Alpha wolf and get him to watch your back."

A noise caught his attention, and he glanced up to spot Cullen standing in the archway leading from the living room to the kitchen. His lover leaned his shoulder against the wall and had one hand tucked into his front pocket.

"Seriously? You want me to do that?" Nash wasn't sure it was the best idea.

"Yes. I'll call back when I know the ETA of our unit in Fallen Creek."

After his boss hung up, Nash set his phone down. He gripped the edge of the counter with both hands while staring down at the floor. What would be the best way to tell Cullen everything? Would Cullen be angry with him because he'd acted like he didn't know anything?

Nash knew he'd probably be pissed if he found out his lover knew all his secrets and didn't share any of that knowledge. Yet Nash understood what his boss was saying. With Union and his goons on their way to Fallen Creek, Nash needed to know someone was there to back him up. He was tough but he couldn't take on five guys on his own.

"Bad news?"

He snorted at Cullen's question. "Yes. You could say that."

Cullen tilted his head back toward the living room. "Do you want to talk about it?"

"As much as I'd prefer not to, I guess I don't have any choice."

Nash pushed away before walking past Cullen, leading the way to the couch. After sitting, he braced his elbows on his knees, trying to work out how to explain things to Cullen in a way the man would understand.

"Well, I guess this means I don't have to spill my guts to you yet," Cullen said, seeming to joke.

"To be honest, Cullen, you don't need to tell me your

secrets at all. I already know them."

"What the hell?"

Cullen's boots appeared in his line of sight, and he looked up to meet Cullen's glare.

Shrugging, Nash smiled for a second then dropped his gaze.

"I've been beating myself up, trying to figure out some way to tell you the truth, and now you claim you know about me?" Cullen said. He flopped onto the couch with a grunt.

Nash rose to his feet, pacing the space in between the couch and the fireplace. He clenched his hands several times before he stopped, turning to face Cullen.

"I was just ordered to tell you everything because it looks like a group of guys are heading to Fallen Creek, ready to kick my ass." Nash frowned. "I wasn't going to tell you anything. I was just going to hang out here for a week or two before I headed out to Santa Monica. That was all true."

Cullen shook his head. "What is it you think you know about me, Nash?"

He took a deep breath then said, "You're a wolf shifter and you've just become the Alpha of Robinson's pack."

Cullen stared at him for several seconds. "Okay," he said slowly. "Well, I guess at least I don't have to worry about you freaking out over the truth." Cullen settled back against the couch. His intense stare reminded Nash of a predator learning the habits of its prey. "How do you know this?"

"I work for an agency that deals with out-of-control shifters. Not just packs, but individuals as well. I was recruited when I was around sixteen."

Nash stopped when Cullen held up his hand.

"Wait."

Nash gave Cullen a questioning glance, waiting for him to continue.

"Are you a shifter?"

Chapter Ten

While he waited for Nash to answer him, Cullen fought the urge to grab Nash and shake him until his teeth rattled. He hated the fact that the man had kept secrets from him, even though he knew it was stupid to feel that way. It wasn't like Nash knew him well enough to trust him completely. He didn't have to trust someone to have sex with him. And it wasn't like he hadn't been keeping his own secrets as well.

Nash pursed his lips while studying the floor.

"It's a simple question, Nash. Are you a shifter or not?"

"Sort of." Nash scrubbed his hand over his face.

"What the hell does 'sort of' mean?"

"I'm half shifter, but we don't know what kind."

Cullen huffed in annoyance. "How can you not know?"

"My father didn't stick around after my mom told him she was pregnant. I can't shift, so we don't have a clue as to what I might be." Nash curled his upper lip while talking about his father.

"Sorry." Cullen was going to let that topic go for now. "Why were you keeping an eye on the motorcycle club?"

"Actually, I was part of the motorcycle club before they recruited me. The agency I'm part of has connections with the DEA and ATF, which was how I ended up in the hospital."

Nash began to pace, causing Cullen to twitch from the guy's nervous movements.

"I don't get it. Is the head of the motorcycle club a shifter or something?"

Nash shook his head. "No. Union is simply a miserable excuse for a human being."

Cullen's head hurt and he wished he could go to bed, bury his head under a pillow, and sleep for an entire day or two. His meeting with Robinson's pack had gone like shit. The members were either junkies or too scared to make any sense. He was going to have to wait for a little while and hope they accepted him. He'd laid down some new laws, but he doubted they were happy about it. The first law was that there would be no more drugs. He wasn't going to allow them to make any, do any, or deliver any. Cullen didn't have a lot of ethics or morals about things, but, since Sara's death, he didn't believe in drugs at all.

He pinched the bridge of his nose and drew a deep breath. "What made this agency of yours decide to look at the club?"

"I was a member and worked for the agency. The other initial agencies had been looking for a way into the club, and they asked my boss if they could borrow me. I moved my way up the chain of command, mostly due to my superior strength, until I became the sergeant-at-arms." Nash glanced over at him. "Are you all right?"

"I had a headache when I came home and it's only getting worse. None of this shit makes sense." Cullen held out his hand to Nash. "Come here and sit next to me."

He wasn't sure if Nash was going to do so or not, but right before he dropped his hand, Nash grabbed it and sat. Cullen wrapped his arm around Nash's shoulder then pulled him close.

"Does this mean you're not mad at me?" Nash rested his head on Cullen's chest.

"At the moment, I don't have the energy to be angry. Maybe after I get some sleep I'll be able to work up a good rage or something."

Nash chuckled. "I guess I should be happy about that. I figured out what you were that night at the bar during the fight. I was going to get you to tell me everything, then act freaked out for a little while before I graciously accepted you. But something's come up, and my boss said I needed to stop all the bullshit."

"I agree with your boss, but if I ever meet him, I'm going to punch him in the face. Why did he send you to Fallen Creek in the first place? Were you supposed to stop Robinson or something?" Cullen leaned back, closing his eyes.

"Nope. I really was on my way to Santa Monica to hang out with Mom for a while. I've worked the motorcycle club case for most of my adult life, and, after I got out of the hospital, I needed to get away from Nashville. It was just good—or bad—luck that I stopped here, depending on how you look at it."

Cullen grunted when Nash pressed his hand to his chest and began to stroke softly.

"When I first arrived, I met Sheriff Carter, and he ended up contacting the Nashville PD about me. We should've known Union would have contacts in the department, but I didn't even think about it."

Nash continued to touch him, and Cullen realized he wanted more than his hand on him.

"Union found out where the star witness for the prosecution is hiding out, which is me, and he's on his way here to take me out. My boss told me to tell you everything so that I could ask you to back me up when Union gets here. My agency already knew about your challenge to Robinson and that you became the Alpha of the pack here."

Cullen pushed Nash back a little so he could look at the man's eyes. "Even if you didn't tell me about who you really are, I'd have helped you out. You're my lover, Nash, and I wouldn't let anyone hurt you if I could help it."

"I really don't need you to protect me," Nash pointed out.

"True, but you do need someone to be your partner and to have your back when the bastards get here. I'll do that. Also, we should probably alert all those agencies you were working with as well."

Nash slipped his hand under Cullen's T-shirt to tease Cullen's belly button. Cullen started trailing his fingers through Nash's hair.

"It's been done, but my boss doesn't think anyone will get here in time to help out. I'm pretty sure they'll be doing the clean-up." Nash brushed a kiss over Cullen's ear.

"Yes, they will, but unfortunately, it's just going to be you and me. My pack is full of useless cowards and druggies. None of whom will do anything except piss themselves if asked to fight."

Cullen tipped his head, letting Nash trail his lips down his neck. He sucked in his stomach when Nash took a hold of his jeans to start unbuttoning them.

"Packs tend to do as the Alpha orders them." Nash slowly sank to his knees, shoving Cullen's pants down to his thighs.

"I know, but my pack isn't a normal group of shifters. They've spent most of their lives abused by Robinson, until they wouldn't risk doing anything for fear of angering him."

He let his eyes drift closed when Nash wrapped his mouth around the head of Cullen's cock. The heat surrounded his flesh and he bit his lip, trying to keep a moan inside. *Christ!* Nash took him all the way in, burying his nose in Cullen's pubic hair.

Tightening his grip on Nash's head, Cullen held him still while he thrust in and out of Nash's mouth. His lover submitted and rested his hands on Cullen's legs to keep his balance.

"Fuck, you have the most perfect mouth," Cullen forced out.

Nash hummed, and Cullen shuddered as the vibration waved around him. He kept moving, loving the way Nash took all he could give him without any argument or struggle.

Pleasure swirled throughout his body before pooling at the base of his spine. Cullen could feel his climax building, so he tapped the side of Nash's head to warn him. Nash grunted but didn't pull off.

"Shit!"

Cum spilled from Cullen's cock, filling Nash's mouth too fast for the man to swallow all of it. Some dribbled out of the corners and down his chin. Once Nash seemed to have sucked the last drop of his essence out of him, Cullen slumped over, stroking the top of Nash's head and smiling when Nash rested his face against his thigh.

"Do you want me to take care of you, honey?"

Nash crawled into Cullen's lap, straddling his legs before rocking against Cullen's stomach. Cullen gripped one of Nash's hips with his hand and encouraged his lover to move. The stiffness of Nash's erection, plus the groans coming from him, told Cullen it wouldn't be long before Nash came.

He caught Nash's nape with his other hand and brought Nash's lips down to his. Cullen kissed the man, sweeping his tongue into Nash's mouth and tasting himself.

They rocked together as their moans mingled. They moved faster and faster until Nash threw his head back and shouted. Warm liquid splashed onto Cullen's stomach as Nash came.

Cullen encircled Nash's waist, clutching him tightly to his chest. He didn't care about the cum between them. Their heartbeats slowed and their breathing calmed. He stroked his hand up and down Nash's back, finding himself humming softly.

Finally, Nash shifted slightly, and Cullen let him go. After Nash climbed off the couch, he took the hand Nash offered him. They wandered to the bathroom, where they cleaned up before stripping to climb into bed.

"When will the motorcycle guys get here?" Cullen asked, staring at the ceiling.

Nash snuggled close. "Any day now. We should probably go into town and warn the deputies about Union. At least let them know there could be trouble. While I'm working at The Watering Hole, I'll be able to keep an eye out for them as well."

"You'll call me when they show up."

He wasn't going to let Nash face his past alone. He was going to do for Nash what he hadn't been able to do for Sara. Cullen would save Nash, even though Nash would say he didn't need saving.

"Of course I will," Nash said, but the tone of his voice told Cullen he was lying.

"Fine, if you won't tell me, I'll just get Jeanette to tell me instead," he threatened.

Nash snorted but changed the subject. "Aren't you afraid someone in your new pack will challenge you for the Alpha position? By shutting the drug business down, you're losing them a lot of money."

Cullen shrugged, lifting Nash's head with his shoulder. "What they're losing out on more is the drugs themselves. Robinson kept most of the money for himself. He didn't spread the wealth, though that turned out to be a good thing. I went over some of his files today after talking to the pack. Someone convinced the bastard to actually have a pack savings account."

After pushing up on his elbow, Nash frowned down at him. "You're kidding, right? A drug dealing shifter who saves his money? Whoever heard of that?"

"I never have really, but it's good news for the pack. The money will give me the opportunity to help them with education and paying bills until they can get real jobs." Cullen rubbed his hand over his face. "I need to figure out who my Betas will be."

So much work for a job he never wanted.

He grunted when Nash smacked him in the chest. Rubbing the injured spot, he glared at Nash. "What the hell was that for?"

"I'll help you out with finding the Betas. Shit, we could probably call my boss and he'd have ideas. There might be wolves out there that are looking for a pack to join." Nash narrowed his gaze while he seemed to be thinking. "In fact, I know of a couple of wolf shifters who are available. Wolves don't seem to do well without a pack."

Cullen nodded. "Yes. We're much more group-oriented usually."

"Why aren't you, then? I get the feeling you've been a lone wolf most of your life, and if you hadn't had to take Robinson down to protect me and Jeanette, you'd have happily ignored what he'd been doing." Nash nudged him in the stomach.

He swatted Nash's hand away. "You're right. I've known what the pack's been doing since I moved here, but as long as they weren't trespassing on my land, I didn't care. They were only hurting themselves, and the humans who bought the drugs were making their own choices. I learned the hard way that you can't help someone unless they want it. As far as I could see, none of them wanted it."

Nash shot him a quizzical look and Cullen huffed.

"Fine. I'm sure there were a few of them who wanted help, but they were too weak to demand it, or even think about defying the Alpha."

"That's not very fair, is it? The ones who wanted help couldn't go against tradition, which says the Alpha is the leader of the pack. Whatever he says goes," Nash argued.

Cullen was done talking about this. He rolled over on his side, facing away from Nash. "Let's get some sleep. I have ranch and pack shit to do tomorrow. You have to make sure Union hasn't gotten to town earlier than we expected, plus go talk to Sheriff Carter and his deputies about the imminent invasion of his town by motorcycle gang members and federal agents. I'm sure he'll be thrilled with that."

"We're not finished talking about this," Nash said. "But I'll let it go for now."

"Thanks."

Nash's chuckle was muffled as he leaned over to place a kiss on Cullen's shoulder. He thought it would be the last sound he heard until morning, but suddenly Nash poked him in the side.

"What the fuck?" He glared at Nash over his shoulder.

"Do you need to shift and let your wolf out? Maybe run

around a little or something?"

Cullen shook his head. "Not tonight. I'll go out tomorrow after I feed the cattle. It's the easiest way to check the fences."

"All right. Just checking, since you probably haven't shifted as often because you didn't want me to know."

"Fuck off," Cullen mumbled. "I don't stop shifting for anyone. You're a pretty sound sleeper. I just waited until you started snoring and snuck out."

He smiled as Nash spooned him and he heard Nash mutter, "Bastard."

* * * *

Cullen watched Nash wave from the entrance of the bar. He growled low in his throat because his wolf wasn't happy about being separated from the man, but there wasn't anything Cullen could do. They both had a lot to do to prepare for Union's arrival.

He couldn't help but wish the agents would get to Fallen Creek before the motorcycle guys did. He would do whatever was needed to keep Nash safe, but he wasn't interested in being part of another fight, especially if it involved humans.

After pulling out of the parking lot, he drove toward his pack's meeting ground. It was time for another chat with all of them, and to see what they had to say about the laws he'd handed down yesterday.

To be fair, what he'd told Nash last night hadn't been completely true. There were some members in the pack who would step up and do what was right. They were the ones who already had legal jobs or were going to school to give themselves a better chance in the world.

With the money Robinson had stashed away, Cullen planned to help them out. Yet a majority of the wolves had gone along with Robinson's drug business because it was easy money, and once they were hooked on the drugs, it was the best way to get it without too much work. Those were the individuals Cullen wanted out of his pack, and he would do everything he could to push them out.

Unfortunately, no one in the pack was the type he wanted for his Betas. None of them had the strength—mentally or physically—to be able to back him in a fight. They might end up being good people, but it took a certain type of wolf to be a Beta. Maybe he would have to talk to Nash some more and see if he could send for those wolves he'd mentioned.

It was a good thing he liked Fallen Creek and the surrounding area, because it looked like he would be staying for quite some time. Not that he had planned to leave any time soon, but still, he'd always kept his options open. Now he was stuck, running a pack he hadn't wanted, while the man he loved rode away into the sunset.

Cullen pulled into the meeting grounds. He turned his truck off before resting his forehead against the steering wheel. Closing his eyes, he groaned softly. *Fuck!* He couldn't be in love with Nash, not so soon. They hadn't even known each other a week, and yet Cullen was afraid he'd fallen for Nash.

Why? What was it about Nash that made Cullen think of love when no one else had ever done so? How would he know what love was when he'd never been in love before? Sara didn't count because, while Cullen had loved her, it was as a sister, not a lover.

Knocking on the window drew his attention, and he sat up to look. Bradley, one of his new pack members, stood outside the truck, nervously chewing on his bottom lip.

It was time to suck it up and be the Alpha his pack needed. Cullen opened the door and stepped out. Bradley dropped his gaze, tilting his head to bare his neck. Cullen touched Bradley's nape with his fingers, letting the younger wolf know he accepted his submission.

"Is everyone here that I asked for?"

"Yes, sir. They're in the pack building, along with all the files you wanted to look at."

"Good."

Cullen stalked toward the building, with Bradley scrambling to keep up. He walked inside to see the people he'd determined to have been Robinson's inner circle arguing among themselves. He put his arm out to stop Bradley before any of them saw him. When Bradley turned to look at him, he shook his head. He wanted to hear what they were saying.

"Why should we listen to him? He comes in here and tells us we're not going to sell drugs anymore. How the hell are we supposed to pay for our houses?"

"Maybe with a real job that isn't illegal and isn't harmful to other people."

Cullen checked to see who'd said that. It was a bigger blond man Cullen had never seen before. He hadn't been part of the group Cullen had asked to meet him at the pack grounds.

"Yeah, well, not all of us are lucky enough to know people who can get us cushy office jobs like you, Eric," one of the other shifters snarled at him.

Eric curled his upper lip and a low growl issued from his throat. The other wolves dipped their heads in acknowledgment of his strength. Cullen grunted softly. Well, at least he knew who one of his Betas might be — that was, if Eric chose to accept the position.

"I think we should band together and get rid of him."

Cullen was slightly surprised. He didn't think any of them would have the guts to even suggest a coup. He studied the woman who'd said it, marking her image and smell in his mind. He wasn't going to punish her for saying it, but if any of them did think about challenging him, they'd find out why he was the Alpha.

"Shut up, Lavinia. If the Alpha was to hear you say that, he could kill you. Do you want that? Personally, I'd rather give him a try. At least we don't have to worry about him freaking out and trying to kill us. Or raping the women."

Bradley coughed, drawing everyone's attention to where

they stood by the door. The moment they realized it was Cullen, they straightened up and stared at him. Well, glared at him was more like it. All except for Eric, who kept his spot in the back of the crowd but met Cullen's gaze with a respectful dip of his head.

"How long have you been standing there?" Lavinia asked.

"Long enough to know most of you aren't happy about the new rules I've given you." Cullen strolled to the table at the front of the room. He sat in the biggest chair before gesturing to them to sit. "You all need to sit, and I'll hear your issues."

"Alpha, we didn't get a chance to meet the other day. I'm Eric Nelson, and I've been a member of the pack for the last six years."

Eric knelt in front of Cullen before bowing his head. Cullen reached out to tap the nape of Eric's neck. After standing, Eric moved to sit at Cullen's right side.

"Really? I've been living in Fallen Creek for four, and while I didn't spend a lot of time in town or with the pack, I don't remember seeing you around."

Eric frowned. "I've been overseas for most of the time. I work for a private contractor that has jobs in foreign countries. Had no idea what the fuck was going on with this pack."

"Is your family a part of the pack?" Cullen ignored the others.

"No, sir. I followed a friend out here and decided to join the pack. I didn't realize then how bad things were. If I had, I wouldn't have become part of it." Eric shook his head. "My family pack isn't perfect, but they weren't this bad."

Cullen snorted. "I never had a pack. My parents chose to wander the country without joining any."

"Not sure this was the best pack to start with as your first," Eric joked.

"You're probably right. I'd like to talk to you about something after the meeting."

"Yes, sir."

Turning back to the others, he stared at them and kept track of who didn't drop their gazes when their eyes met. For wolves and wolf shifters, staring was a sign of aggression.

Lavinia and one male met his gaze boldly until he bared his teeth in a dominant display. They looked down, but his growl brought their gazes back up.

"Remember this. I am the Alpha now and what I say is the law. If you have any objections, then I suggest you tell me now. You won't change my mind about the making or dealing of drugs."

Cullen leaned back in the chair, folding his arms over his chest as he stared at them.

"None of us have any way of making money. We have no talents or skills," Bradley pointed out.

"You'll have to figure something else out, because I won't allow any more illegal activities. Trust me when I say you don't want to see what I'd do to any pack member I find dealing drugs from this moment on." Cullen gritted his teeth as he fought back his anger.

"Why don't we see about the children and make sure they're doing all right in school?" Eric spoke up.

Cullen nodded. "I think Lavinia would be a good person to head up that project. I want to know how each child is doing in school and, if they need help, what we can do for them."

Lavinia didn't look thrilled, but Cullen didn't care. All that mattered was that she learned to do as she was told without arguing about everything. He didn't mind being questioned when or if one of his members had doubts—however, he wasn't going to allow them to question his ability to lead the pack.

"Fine, sir." She started to stand, but a low growl from Cullen froze her in her seat.

"You may leave when I excuse you, Lavinia. Remember who is in charge here, even if you'd like to challenge me." Cullen looked each person in the eye. "All of you remember who I am. I might not be who you'd prefer as your Alpha, but I am the head of this pack, and things are going to be far different here from now on."

Bradley and most of the others shrank back, letting him know they were submissive. Lavinia lowered her eyes, obviously not wanting to submit but knowing she must.

He gestured for all of them to sit. "Now let's discuss some other ways we can make this pack one to be proud of, and not a laughingstock among the other packs."

Chapter Eleven

"Have you talked to Deputy Barker yet?"

Nash looked up from where he sat in Jeanette's office. He'd been going over her supply lists to figure out what else was needed to be able to re-open the bar. He smiled when he saw Cullen leaning in the doorway.

"No. He wasn't in when I went by the sheriff's department. I left a message for him to call me, but he hasn't done it yet." Nash pushed his chair away from the desk before he stood.

Cullen watched him approach with a dark, intense gaze. Something in Cullen's expression caught Nash's attention and he reached out to hook his finger through one of Cullen's belt loops. He tugged the cowboy into the room.

He managed to shut the door behind Cullen, locking it before he shoved Cullen back against the wall. Cullen didn't say a word, he just let Nash push him around. Of course, the man probably wasn't going to say no to whatever Nash had planned.

After dropping to his knees, he tore Cullen's jeans open. Cullen shifted his hips, getting the denim down around his knees. Nash hummed in appreciation as Cullen's cock was revealed. He rubbed his cheek along the length of Cullen's shaft. Cullen growled low in his throat before running his hand over Nash's hair.

Unfortunately, right as he was about to take Cullen in as far as he could, a knock sounded on the door.

"You two better not be doing anything in my office," Jeanette said through the door.

Cullen let his head drop back hard against the wall. Chuckling, Nash climbed to his feet.

"We wouldn't dream of it, Jeanette. Just a second." He gestured for Cullen to pull his pants up.

"Interfering woman," Cullen muttered as he fastened his pants.

When he was done, he unlocked the door. Nash was back at the desk and picked up the list. Jeanette stood there, arms folded, studying them. Nash fought the urge to drop his chin and kick the floor like a naughty schoolboy being disciplined by the head nun.

"Here's the list of supplies we still need to get before you can open back up." Nash handed the list to Jeanette.

She looked it over and sighed. "This is a lot of money."

Cullen took the paper from her. "I'll take care of this. Robinson caused the problem, and I have access to the pack's accounts. Trust me. The pack has more than enough money to cover this."

"Really? I didn't think the pack had anything. At least, it didn't look like they did." Jeanette looked at him.

"Turns out Robinson banked most of his cut. Maybe he planned on leaving at some point, but not taking the pack with him. Perhaps he was going to cut and run, and the money was his safety net." Cullen shrugged. "I told the pack there'd be no more drugs—dealing or making. Also, no doing them either."

"Bet that went over well," Nash commented.

Cullen rolled his eyes. "It doesn't matter what they think about my rules. I'm the Alpha and what I say goes. I laid down a few more rules today with the inner circle. I also think I've found one of my Betas. He seems like a good guy."

"Shit! I forgot to call the guys I know. Do you still need them?"

"Yeah. See if they're willing to come here. I'll meet with them and see if they'll fit in."

Nash made a mental note to do that later. He joined Cullen by the door before he looked at Jeannette.

"I have to talk to Deputy Barker about some shit that's

coming here. You should know about it as well. I was part of a DEA and ATF case in Nashville. The motorcycle club I was a member of dealt in a lot of bad shit, and I helped the Feds to get proof on them." Nash rubbed the back of his neck then pressed his hand to his side. "Union figured out I was the snitch and he had some of the guys beat the shit out of me. I was in the hospital for a couple months."

"Is he on his way here?" Jeanette sounded urgent.

Nash shot Cullen a quick glance, then looked at Jeanette. "Yes. He and some of his men are. They found out where I'd stopped and now he's coming to finish what they started."

Jeanette took a deep breath before hugging him. "Thank you for telling me. I'll keep an eye out for any strangers. If they show up here, I'll get a hold of you. You're not alone with this, Nashville. Cullen has your back. I can't think of any other guy I'd want there more."

Nash agreed. Cullen didn't say much and didn't seem to need anyone. The closer he grew to Cullen, the more Nash learned that Cullen was loyal to the bone. If a person was a friend of his, he'd go to the ends of the earth to save them.

But Cullen was a tough S.O.B. and, being a wolf, he'd be hard to take down. Having come to care a great deal for Cullen, Nash didn't want to have to visit him in the hospital.

"I know, Jeanette. Why do you think I've told him about all of it? He's the only one, besides my friend Ten, who I'd trust to back me up when I need it." Nash didn't even think about it. He pushed up on his toes and pressed a kiss to Cullen's lips. "Strange to think we've only known each other for a few days. I'd let you hold my life in your hands."

Cullen grunted but didn't back away from him. Nash wasn't entirely sure what Cullen thought about the whole situation. Now wasn't the time to discuss the future, or maybe they shouldn't discuss anything at all. Just let things play out as they would, to an ending Nash couldn't see.

"Now get out of here. There's nothing to do at the moment. Why don't you let me place the order, Cullen, and I'll get you the bill?" Jeanette took the list from Cullen.

"All right. You know better than I do what the good stuff is, and how to haggle for reasonable prices. I'll take Nash to see the deputy, then we'll probably go out to the ranch. Call if you need us." Cullen tilted his head in the direction of the front of the bar.

Nash didn't really want to talk to the police. If he had to kill Union and his men, he would. The shifter group he worked for would take care of cleaning the mess up.

Nodding, Nash strolled to the entrance. He waited for Cullen to catch up before he stepped outside. Cullen rested his hand on his shoulder, stopping him in the bar. He looked up into Cullen's dark eyes.

"I will do everything in my power to keep you safe," Cullen promised, his voice thick and slightly emotional.

Nash cradled Cullen's face in his hands and smiled. "I know you will. We're men. We don't talk about our feelings, and, hell, we haven't known each other that long, but I can tell you won't leave me. Hopefully, we'll get through this without either of us getting hurt."

Cullen's gaze shifted to the side and he swallowed audibly. "I let down someone close to me and she died. I told myself I'd never do that again. Of course, I told myself I'd never get close enough to anyone to be put in that position."

"Then I arrived," Nash said.

"Yes. You came riding in on your motorcycle and roared into a space in my heart I didn't even know existed. I'm not going to say anything right now, but I hope, when this problem with Union is solved, you'll think about sticking around for a while longer. I know you want to visit your mother and everything. Maybe you won't want to stay in a backward town like Fallen Creek."

Nash placed his finger on Cullen's lips to stop his babbling. Nash's heart beat faster, not from fear but from excitement. He had a feeling he knew Cullen cared about him, and even if he never got the words, he'd be happy to spend the rest of his life with Cullen.

"You're right. We don't have to talk about this right now.

Once Union is dealt with, we'll discuss me staying on a little longer. It'll depend more on where the group I work for wants me than me wanting to leave."

He really did hope Cullen understood that if he had to leave, it wouldn't be because he wanted to. Cullen kissed Nash's finger then nodded.

"All right. Then let's go and get this meeting with the police over with. This spot between my shoulder blades is itching, which usually means something's going to happen soon. I want the police ready for it."

Nash pushed open the door to step outside. Cullen's growl hit his ears at the same time as Nash spotted Union standing next to his bike.

"Look...if it isn't the fag snitch. Glad I didn't have to search this whole podunk town for your ass." Union sneered at him, leaning against Nash's bike.

The other two men with Union stood two steps behind him, one to the right and the other to the left. They had their arms folded over their chests and their feet spread wide. Nash wasn't surprised to see Hawk and Rat were there. They were the two closest to Union. His right-hand men who did all of his personal dirty work.

"What are you doing here, Union?" Nash stepped closer to Union.

He felt the warmth from Cullen's body as his lover moved with him. Fear did swirl inside Nash, but Cullen's presence helped him get a hold of it. It was all right to be afraid. He just couldn't let any of it show or Union would be on him like a wolf on a deer.

Cullen growled and Nash squared his shoulders to face Union.

"I see you found a new cocksucker. Does he fuck you or do you take it up the ass?" Union curled his upper lip in contempt.

At some point in the past, Nash might have protested Union's words simply to keep up appearances, but spending those months in the hospital, then being with Cullen, had shown him he needed to be honest with himself. And that meant being truthful with everyone around him.

"It's none of your business who I spend my time with, Union. I'm not a member of your club anymore. Not that there's any club to be a part of." Nash clenched his hands.

"Oh yeah, there's still a club, Rhodes. As long as I'm still alive, there'll always be a club. I've never wanted you to be a member because I thought you were weak. Not surprised to find out you're queer."

"Saw how you used to look at me. Should've known you wanted me," Rat bragged, nudging Hawk with his elbow.

Hawk didn't say a word, but he edged a few inches away from Rat. Nash knew Hawk didn't like Rat, so he wasn't shocked Hawk wanted nothing to do with the man.

"Is Nash blind?" Cullen spoke up.

"No," Rat replied. "Why ask that?"

"Because the only way Nash would ever want you would be if he couldn't see you. Although, he could still smell, and you reek. You should really take a shower once in a while, asshole."

Nash glanced over at Cullen to see his lover had wrinkled his nose. He couldn't help it—he burst into laughter.

"Who are you laughing at, you queers?" Rat shouted as he sprinted toward them.

Cullen pushed past him and Nash let him go. He wouldn't worry about his lover. Cullen could take care of himself. Nash didn't think Rat or Hawk had silver bullets.

"While they're taking care of your cock-sucking buddy, I'll be dealing with you." Union cracked his knuckles like a B-movie bad guy.

"Wait a minute."

All the men froze at Jeanette's shout. After turning, Nash saw Jeanette standing on the front steps with a shotgun held in her arms.

"You won't be doing it in front of my place. Take the brawl out back. At least there'll be less chance of collateral damage." Jeanette jerked her head in the direction of the back of the bar.

"Seriously? You've got to be fucking kidding me." Union rolled his eyes as he reached for Nash's shoulder.

Jeanette cocked the hammer on the gun before pointing it right at Union. "Hell, yes, I'm serious. I won't have you beating the shit out of each other in my parking lot. I've managed to keep the police from dropping in here, and I don't want them getting familiar with this place unless they're here to drink."

"Ow! Hey, let go of me!"

Nash glanced over to see Cullen dragging Rat by the collar of his leather jacket. The biker fought every step of the way, but he obviously wasn't even making Cullen work for it. Hawk followed behind them, yet something in the set of his shoulders made Nash think the man wasn't interested in getting in the middle of Rat and Cullen.

"What do you say, Union? You want to kick my ass so bad. The only way you're going to be able to have a chance is if we go back there." Nash shot Union a disrespectful glance. "Not that I'm saying you can do it. Trust me. I'm tougher than I look."

"Bullshit. I'm going to hand you your ass. Your boyfriend better get a good look at you because by the time I'm done with you, you won't be nearly as cute as you are now." Union sneered.

Nash strolled around the building to where he found Cullen pinning Rat to the ground with his hand wrapped around Rat's throat.

"Oh, hey, Cullen, did you hear? Union thinks I'm pretty. Maybe I should've asked him out. Sounds like he might be interested in sucking my dick."

Cullen looked up, but Nash didn't need to see the warning in Cullen's eyes to know Union was coming up behind him. He ducked the roundhouse punch Union had thrown at his head.

"Should've known you wouldn't fight fair, Union."

Nash grabbed Union's arm to jerk the man forward into

his fist. Union doubled over, clutching his stomach. Nash started to move in for the kill, but his foot landed on a rock and his ankle twisted.

He went down and Union recovered enough to come after him. He grunted as Union landed on him, knees driving into his stomach. All the air rushed out of Nash's lungs and he fought back the tears welling in his eyes.

Fuck! His ribs were never going to be the same after this. He was sure another one of them had cracked. After taking a handful of sand, he threw it into Union's face.

"God damn." Union scrubbed at his eyes.

Nash slammed his feet into Union's solar plexus with as much force as he could muster. While Union rolled on the ground, Nash stood. After drawing his leg back, he kicked Union in the side, aiming for the kidney.

Their fight disintegrated into punches and kicks. Each one landed serious blows, and it felt like there wasn't any advantage for either. Nash was glad he didn't have to worry about Cullen. His lover would do whatever he had to do to keep the other two from joining the fight.

Unfortunately, the injuries Nash had been recovering from were wearing him down faster than normal. Usually his half-shifter blood kept him from ending up badly hurt, or worse. It also helped him win all of his fights.

This time, though, it wasn't helping. He could feel his strength waning. He needed to end this fight or it would be too late.

"Nash, watch out."

Cullen's warning came in time as Union rushed him, holding a knife. Nash turned to the side, but he didn't get completely out of the way. The blade sliced through the flesh at his side and he shouted in pain.

"That's it. Enough."

Cullen's roar shook the buildings around them and froze Union in his tracks. Nash dropped to his knees, holding his side, but kept watching as Cullen grabbed Union's fist in his hand and squeezed until Union screamed in agony.

The knife dropped to the dirt, with Union close behind. Snarling, Cullen leaned over the biker, almost like he was going to take a chunk out of him. Cullen's eyes were glowing and his canines were growing into fangs. Nash needed Cullen to get a hold of his anger or Union was going to see that some myths really were true.

"Cullen, take a breath. Get control of yourself." Nash looked over to where Hawk stood. "You need to get off your ass and get Union away from Cullen or he'll kill him."

"Are you worried that your boyfriend might kill Union?" Hawk snorted. "I don't think that'll happen. Your boyfriend's got a hold of himself. I think he's just putting the fear of God into Union."

There was a thud, and when Nash looked back, Union lay crumpled on the ground. Cullen stepped over him like he was a piece of garbage. Nash managed a smile as Cullen dropped to his knees next to him.

"Are you all right?"

"My hero," Nash joked.

"Shut up." Cullen pulled out his phone and tossed it at Hawk. "Call nine-one-one. Have them send an ambulance. All three of them need to go to the hospital."

Hawk pointed at himself. "Do I look like I'm your fucking servant?"

"You'll lose that fucking hand if you don't do what I told you." Cullen didn't look at Hawk, but his tone said he meant it.

"I'm getting too fucking old for this shit," Nash murmured as he lifted his hand from where he'd pressed it against his side. He stared at the blood on it. "I'm tired of seeing my own blood."

He heard Hawk talking on the phone, but he focused on Cullen's face. There was fear and anger in his eyes, yet Nash saw something else and it made his heart skip a beat. He wasn't about to call Cullen on it, though. There was still time enough for that.

"I think you need to stop putting yourself into situations

where this kind of shit happens to you." Cullen touched Nash's face with gentle fingers.

"I think you might be right." Nash laughed slightly, the pain making him lose his breath.

"The ambulance and police will be here soon." Hawk walked over to them before handing Cullen back his phone.

"You're not really a part of the club, are you?" Cullen asked the question running around Nash's head.

Hawk laughed. "Yeah, I am, but I haven't liked the way Union's been running it for a while now. It's just loyalty to the rest of the guys means something to me. Of course, I knew you were a rat almost from the moment the DEA got hold of you."

Nash grunted in surprise. "You did? But you didn't say anything to Union about it. Why is that?"

"It was more important to get Union out than to worry about what the hell you were doing. The club will continue, just as something better than what Union has turned it into. I plan on taking over as president and taking it legitimate." Hawk pursed his lips as he stared out over the yard. "It'll take a lot of work and maybe we'll need to relocate."

Cullen growled low in his throat, causing both Nash and Hawk to look at him. "You can't move here. There's only room for one pack, and I already claim Fallen Creek as mine."

Hawk chuckled. "Man, I don't think any of my guys would move here. It's out of the way from everything. There's not enough business for us to open a garage or anything either."

"Good. I don't want any more strangers coming into my town and messing things up." Cullen snarled.

"Wait. Will you allow Ten back into the club? He didn't have anything to do with what I did. He's just been my best friend forever." He wanted to make sure Ten had a home to go back to if he wanted to go.

"Sure. He disappeared right before we headed out here, but I figured it was because he was going to warn you.

Didn't care if he did or not. You did what you thought you had to do and, well, it suited my goals to let you do so. Ten's a good guy. I might have a place in my inner circle for him, if he wants."

Hawk hesitated, and Nash blinked as he tried to keep his eyes from blurring. He turned to look at Cullen, who was stripping off his shirt. Cullen folded it into a pad then put it against Nash's wound.

Nash hissed in pain as Cullen pushed against it.

"Sorry, Nash. I have to stop the bleeding or you're going to lose consciousness at some point. The EMTs will be here shortly." Cullen ground his teeth, and Nash could see his injury was really worrying Cullen.

He patted Cullen's arm. "Don't worry. I'll be all right. Just another scar to add to all the others, though my ribs will never be the same again."

"Ten will have to decide if he wants to come back to the club." Hawk rolled his eyes. "I'll do my best to make sure no one hassles him, but I can't guarantee the men won't give him trouble for being Union's nephew and your friend."

"Well, that's big of you," Cullen snapped. "If Ten decides he doesn't want to be part of the club anymore, we'll take him here."

"I'll let him know about your offer." Hawk nodded.

The sirens grew closer then stopped. Nash gripped Cullen's arm to get his attention.

"Find my phone and call my mother. Let her know what happened. She's not going to be happy with me. She yelled at me for an hour when she came to the hospital during my first stay. Mom's going to be pissed and on a plane here within minutes of hanging up." Nash bit his bottom lip as a spasm of pain rippled through him.

Cullen's eyes widened at Nash's request. Apparently, the thought of meeting Nash's mother terrified Cullen.

"Are you afraid of a little old lady? I swear she won't bite or anything." He paused for a moment before continuing, "Mom might hit you some for letting her little boy get injured, but she'll forgive you once she figures out we're sleeping together."

Redness colored Cullen's cheeks, and Nash chuckled again.

"Are you blushing? Really? You're blushing because my mom is going to know we had sex?" Nash shook his head. "She's not dumb. The moment she sees the two of us together, she'll know."

"Christ! I don't think I can look the woman in the face if she's going to talk to me about having sex with you." Cullen looked ill at the thought of talking—or even thinking—about sex in the same thought as Nash's mother.

Chapter Twelve

Cullen looked up to see the EMTs and sheriff's deputies come racing around the corner of the building. He growled as they approached him, but Nash tightened his grip to get Cullen's attention.

"Let them do their job, Cullen. It'll be all right."

He backed off, though every instinct in his body told him to protect Nash. There wasn't anything he could do for Nash, and the EMTs were far more capable of helping him.

"Cullen, what the hell happened here?" Deputy Barker yelled to him.

After standing, Cullen turned to find that the deputy had Rat and Union in cuffs. Hawk stood next to his motorcycle buddies, but he wasn't restrained. The cuffed men both looked the worse for wear.

"We were actually on our way over to tell you about the problem when these assholes showed up." Cullen stalked over and snarled at them.

"Fine, but who are they? I heard some bikers rode into town this morning, but I didn't think they'd come to beat the shit out of you and Rhodes there." Barker didn't look happy.

Who could blame him? First, Sheriff Carter had almost been killed by Robinson's gang while trying to stop a bar fight. Now three strangers, two of whom had obviously had the shit beaten out of them, had come to town and threatened one of its citizens.

"You should be asking for a raise, Barker. I bet you thought you'd have a pretty easy time of it while Carter was recovering." Cullen couldn't help but joke.

"Shut the fuck up, Cullen. Just tell me what the hell happened." Barker yanked out his notebook and a pencil.

Cullen checked on Nash and saw the EMTs were doing fine without him. When he heard Nash gasp, Cullen swung around to grab the front of Union's blood-soaked shirt. He shook him hard once.

"If they ever let you out of prison, I don't want to see your face around here again. Or else I'll kill you."

"Cullen, let go of him."

Barker grabbed him, trying to pull him away from Union. Of course, the human didn't have the strength to stop Cullen from doing anything he wanted. He didn't want to kill Union, though. He simply wanted to reinforce the threat.

"Cullen, if you don't let go, I'm going to have to arrest you as well," Barker warned.

"Fine."

Cullen let go, and Union dropped to his knees again. After glaring at Rat, Cullen met Barker's irritated gaze.

"Nash was part of a motorcycle club in Nashville. He cooperated with some federal agencies to get enough evidence on the members to send quite a few of them to prison for a long while. After he healed from the beating I'm pretty sure this bastard gave him"—Cullen nudged Union with the toe of his boot—"he headed out to visit his mother. Decided to stop here, and, somehow, Union found him. I'm pretty sure Nash'll have the number of someone you can contact about the whole thing."

"We're transporting him to the hospital, Cullen." One of the EMTs walked over to let Cullen know. "He wanted you to have this. Said don't forget to call his mother."

Cullen swallowed and instantly became annoyed. He was the Big Bad Wolf, for Christ's sake! Why did the thought of talking to and seeing Nash's mother make him quiver in fear? She was just one lady, and Cullen had dealt with scarier people throughout his life. Yet the idea of Nash's mother knowing about him having sex with her son made

Cullen weak in the knees. It actually made him physically ill to imagine how that conversation would go.

"I'll follow you there." He faced Barker. "If you want more, you know where to find me."

He left without hearing anything else Barker had to say. He wasn't interested in being yelled at by the deputy about not letting him know sooner about Union and the others. Hell, it wasn't his story to tell, and they had been on their way to explain things to him. It was just that the situation had gotten out of hand before anything could be said.

When he rounded the corner of the building, he saw Jeanette leaning over Nash at the back of the ambulance. What was the meddling woman up to now? Cullen still hadn't figured out what she was—although she certainly wasn't human, she didn't smell like any other shifter Cullen had scented before.

"Get away from him, woman. He needs to get to the hospital." Cullen stomped up to them.

She waggled her finger at him. "You didn't do a very good job of keeping Nash from getting hurt again."

How did she know just the right button to push to make Cullen feel guilty? He fought the need to hang his head and kick at the dirt.

"Don't scold him, Jeanette. He couldn't have known Union would pull a knife, though I should've. He's never fought a fair fight in his life."

Nash's pupils were blown, so Cullen knew his lover was flying high on the painkillers the EMTs had given him. Cullen patted Nash's shoulder.

"Let them get you to the hospital. I'll be right behind you."

He wanted to lean down and kiss Nash, but he wasn't about to do that in front of all these people. Not that he was ashamed about his relationship with Nash. He just didn't know whom he could trust not to take their bigoted homophobia out on a wounded man.

A guy could seem like a nice person until he was confronted by something he thought was an abomination or a sin. That was part of the reason why Cullen never said anything about being a shifter. Too big a risk.

"I'm coming with you. You shouldn't be sitting in the waiting room alone, and I want to make sure Nash is all right."

"Fine. Come on then."

He didn't watch Nash get loaded into the back of the ambulance. After climbing into his truck, he waited for Jeanette to secure the bar then get her seatbelt fastened before taking off after Nash.

Cullen managed to stay just under the speed limit as he followed the emergency vehicle. Jeanette didn't say anything to him while he drove, and he was thankful for that. He didn't feel like talking about anything right then.

They pulled into the parking lot, and after he'd parked, they dashed into the building. The lady at the reception desk told them to go up to the surgical floor. After flopping into one of the waiting room chairs, he braced his elbows on his knees and sighed.

Jeanette sat next to him then patted him on the shoulder. "It'll be all right. Nash will get through the surgery and live to fight another day."

"I know, Jeanette. Fate wouldn't be that cruel to me to take him so soon after we met." Cullen growled before continuing, "I have to call his mother and I'm not looking forward to that conversation."

"How bad can it be? She's probably a really nice lady." Jeanette laughed.

"She'd have to be to have a son like Nash, but she's going to want to know if we're together." Cullen shook his head.

Jeanette patted Cullen's back again. "Honey, don't worry about it. She's just looking out for her son, and also, she probably likes to freak out Nash's boyfriends as well."

"You're not helping," he muttered.

"I'm not trying to. Now, it's time to pull on your big boy pants and give Nash's mother a call. She needs to know what's happened to her son. Also, that there are people here who care about him." Jeanette nudged him.

Cullen heaved a sigh then pulled Nash's phone from his pocket. After standing, he strolled outside to sit on one of the benches and turned the phone on before scrolling through Nash's contacts. Stopping at *Mom*, he stared at the number for a few minutes.

"You're a big, tough Alpha, O'Murphy. One lady shouldn't have you shaking in your boots," he mumbled.

With a rush of courage, he hit the call button and held the phone to his ear.

"Nashville, darling, how are you doing? What kind of boy doesn't call his mother every day?" a female voice with a beautiful, honeyed drawl asked.

Cullen almost dropped the phone but managed to get it back before Nash's mother could say anything else.

"Ma'am, my name is Cullen O'Murphy, and I'm calling on Nash's behalf."

"Cullen O'Murphy? You're that cowboy who's been sleeping with my boy."

His face heated and he fought the urge to duck his head, even though she wasn't around to see him do it.

"Yes, ma'am."

"Are you calling to ask for my permission to date my son? It's a little old-fashioned, but I appreciate it." She laughed.

"Umm...ma'am," he interrupted. He wasn't sure how to go about breaking the news to her.

"Please call me Edith, and I have a feeling this isn't a social call." She grew quiet.

"No, Edith, it's not. Unfortunately, Nash was wounded in an altercation here in Fallen Creek. He's in surgery right now, but, as far as I know, he'll be fine." Cullen decided just to spill it all at once.

"God damn it!"

Cullen did pull the phone away from his ear to stare at it for a second. It was strange to hear such a refined lady swear.

"Don't worry, Edith. He'll be fine."

Edith snorted. "I'm sure he will be, but that boy needs to stop getting his ass kicked. And where were you? If you care for Nashville, why didn't you stop him from getting hurt?"

"I'm sorry. I stopped the man before he could hurt Nash any further, but he was holding his own until Union pulled a knife on him. I can't fight every battle for him, no matter how much I might want to." Cullen hated how guilty Edith chewing him out made him feel.

"I know my Nashville, and it doesn't surprise me that he took Union on by himself. I'm glad you were there to back him up, though, even if he did end up injured." Edith sighed. "Here I was thinking that stopping at a small town in Wyoming would be a good place for Nashville to heal and rest up."

Cullen wanted to say he was sorry again. He rolled his eyes then said, "I assume you'd like to come out here and check on Nash yourself. Do you want me to arrange a flight for you? I can do that, then call you back with the flight number and time."

"Yes, I'd better come out to see that boy. He's going to get into more trouble if I don't read him the riot act." Edith heaved a sigh. "I'll make all the reservations and call you to let you know when I get into Cheyenne. You can come get me or send someone to pick me up."

"I'll do that." He hesitated for a second then said, "I'll give you a call when he gets out of surgery and after I've talked to the doctor. That way you will know how it turns out."

"Thank you, Cullen. I appreciate you being there. But don't think you've gotten out of talking about Nashville and your intentions toward him. My son isn't innocent or a virgin, but he's a good man. I won't let you hurt him if you aren't serious about him."

She hung up before he could say anything else. He ended the call then stuffed the phone in his pocket. Cullen stared at the ground, trying to figure out just how he was going to face an older woman who seemed to have no problem discussing her gay son's sex life.

For the first time, Cullen found himself a little happy that his mother was dead. He had the strange feeling she would be like Edith, and the two of them together would wreak havoc on his and Nash's relationship.

"How did it go?"

He glanced up to see Jeanette standing in front of him. Cullen shrugged.

"It wasn't as bad as I thought it would be, but I distracted her when I told her about Nash. I'm sure it'll be worse once she gets here and sees for herself that he's okay." He shook his head.

Jeanette patted him on the head, and he got the feeling she wasn't as sympathetic as she seemed.

"You think this is funny, huh?"

She grinned at him. "Yes, I do. It's hilarious to see a big, badass man scared of a little old lady. Not that Edith is old or anything like that. She's quite spry."

"Do you know her?" He eyed Jeanette with a narrow-eyed gaze. "Have you met her before, Jeanette?"

After sitting next to him, she stared at the building in front of them. "I've never actually met her face to face, but I've known about her for a while. Been hoping to accidentally run into her or Nash at some point."

"Accidentally? Or do you mean accidentally on purpose?" He settled back on the bench to listen to Jeanette's explanation.

"Oh, completely on purpose, but it had to appear accidental. I can't let them know about me yet."

"So you've been hanging around Fallen Creek for years, waiting for the day Nash rode in. That's long-term planning." He couldn't see anyone having the patience to hang out at The Watering Hole, expecting a person to show up.

"Umm...actually, even though you all think I've been here for years, I showed up here about four months ago. I passed a glamor over the town."

He straightened and stared at her. "You're fucking kidding? What the hell are you, Jeanette? You don't smell like a shifter or any other paranormal being I've run into."

When Jeanette turned to look at him, her eyes glowed a strange silver color. He blinked, having truly never seen anyone whose eyes looked like that.

"I'm a fae, Cullen."

Fae? Holy shit!

"You're joking right? The fae are extinct. Disappeared centuries ago." He'd never met a fae, and he'd lived a long time.

"Well, for the most part, we are extinct. Our magic was dependent on belief and faith. We lived in Ireland and rarely traveled off the island. Once Christianity became a viable religion in Ireland, we faded away." Sadness shone in her eyes.

"Why the hell are you here? I can't think that America would be the best place for you." Cullen waved his hand in a vague circle.

Jeanette stood to pace the sidewalk in front of them. "We had to leave Ireland, so we came here. It's not a bad place for us to hide out among the people. As strange as it may sound, there are a lot of believers here. More than are in Europe anymore."

"Fine, but why here and why Nash?" He still didn't understand why Jeanette was interested in Nash and his mother.

"At some point in her family tree, one of Edith's ancestors had a child with a fae."

Shock rippled through Cullen. "How did that happen?"

Jeanette snorted. "The usual way, I assume."

He rolled his eyes. "I know that part. I meant how would a human hook up with one of you? From what I've read about your kind, you didn't like mortals."

She burst out laughing. "Sweetheart, while we did think humans were below us, we still enjoyed having sex with them. So it's not that big a stretch to discover half-fae, half-human offspring."

"And one of Edith's great-great-great-whatevers slept with a fae. You're here to find out or to talk to them about it?" A thought hit him. "Shit! Then Nash is half shifter with some fae blood mixed in. He's quite the smorgasbord of DNA." Cullen shook his head.

"Right. To be honest, there are very few of us left, and even one with diluted blood is better than none at all. Nash needs to know about his entire heritage, not just what he thinks he knows."

"I suggest not dropping it on him right away. He's going to need some time to recover after this last injury. Maybe before his mother leaves, you could sit them down and discuss it with them both."

As much as finding out Jeanette was a member of an endangered paranormal race surprised him, Cullen didn't want Nash bothered right away. He wanted his lover to heal as much as possible before discovering anything else new about himself.

"I can wait a little while longer." Jeanette looked at him. "I thought you'd be more upset to find out I'd put a glamor on you. You seem to have taken that better than I imagined."

Cullen shrugged while he stood. He offered his arm to Jeanette. "It didn't hurt me physically, and there's nothing I can do about it now, right?"

She nodded.

"Then there's no point in getting upset. Hell, I have bigger things to worry about at the moment."

They strolled back inside the hospital to the elevators. Jeanette squeezed his forearm as they went into the elevator car.

"You do seem to have a lot to deal with. How's the pack doing? Any challenges yet?"

He gritted his teeth for a second. "There are going to be a few problems, but I'll handle them. None of them are stronger than me, though one of them might be close. I'm going to do some background inquiries to see if there's anything I should be worried about with him."

Cullen didn't want to think about the pack. He had Edith's arrival to look forward to, along with finding out how Nash had weathered his surgery. When they got back to the waiting room, he went up to the desk to talk to the nurse.

"I'm here for Nashville Rhodes and I was wondering if there's been any news about him. I stepped out to call his mother."

The nurse checked her list. "No, sir. Nothing so far. He must still be in surgery."

God, he hated waiting. He grunted his thanks then went back to sit next to Jeanette. He lost track of time as he found himself praying Nash would be all right.

"Cullen." Jeanette nudged him with her elbow.

He glanced up to see Eric and a few other pack members standing in front of him.

"We heard what happened and we thought we'd come down to see if there's anything we can do," Eric replied to Cullen's unspoken question.

Cullen stood and offered his hand to Eric. "Thanks. I appreciate you coming down. At the moment, we can't do anything except wait for the surgeon to come out."

Eric nodded. "Makes sense, but if you need anything, just give me a call. I'll be glad to help you out."

A thought hit Cullen. "You know, there is something you could do for me. How good are you at dealing with animals?"

"It's not my favorite thing to do, which is why I don't work on any of the ranches around here, but if you need me to, I'll take care of yours." Eric didn't look excited.

"Yeah. I'm sorry, but I'm going to need you to feed them and make sure everything's all right with them." He waved his hand in a vague circle. "I don't know how long I'm going to be here. Once Nash is out of surgery, I don't want to leave until he's awake. Then I'll probably have to run into Cheyenne to pick up Nash's mom."

"Sure, Cullen, I'm more than happy to do it. If I need help, I can get some of the pack to lend a hand."

Cullen nodded. "If any of them give you a hard time, tell them they'll deal with me. You're my Beta, Eric, if you want the job like we talked about."

"I'll take it. I have a feeling the pack is going to be a lot different with you as the Alpha."

"Not sure about that, but hell, it couldn't get any worse, could it?" Cullen smiled slightly.

Nash's phone rang and, after pulling it out his pocket, Cullen checked the screen. It was Nash's mother.

"I have to take this. Jeanette, can you tell Eric how to get out to my ranch?" Cullen took one of his house keys off his ring before holding it out to Eric. "Here's the key to my house. You'll find everything you need in the barn."

Eric took it and went with Jeanette. Cullen wandered off into a corner and answered the phone.

"Hello, Edith."

"Cullen, I wanted to give you my flight number. Will someone be able to meet me at the airport?"

"Yes, ma'am. I'll be sending a friend to pick you up. I don't want to leave Nash alone until he's awake and conscious." Cullen wasn't sure if Edith would be happy about having a stranger get her. Cullen planned to send Eric.

If Eric was going to be his Beta, he would have to deal with issues like picking up his Alpha's boyfriend's mother. Especially when said Alpha wasn't sure he was ready to talk to the woman face to face.

"Sounds good to me. Here's my flight number and when I'll be landing."

He memorized the numbers and time so he could tell Eric.

"Have you heard anything about Nash?" she asked.

"Not yet. The moment I hear anything, I'll call you. I promise."

"I know you will. You seem very determined to watch over my son, and I do appreciate it. I know Nash will as well."

They said goodbye and Cullen hung up before tucking the phone away. He dragged his hand through his hair then turned to see Eric just about to leave the waiting room.

"Eric, wait. I need you to do something else for me. See if you can get some pack members you trust to look after my cattle, then go to Cheyenne. Nash's mother will be coming in late tonight. I told her I'd send a friend to pick her up."

Eric narrowed his eyes. "This is a way for you not to have to face the parent for a while longer, right?"

Jeanette shook her head. "A big, tough man like Cullen and he's doing everything he can to get out of spending time with Nash's mother."

"Hey, mothers can be pretty intimating," Eric joked. "I've met a few, and they were rather scary."

"Fuck off, both of you. I simply don't want to leave Nash's side. Edith understands." Cullen ground his teeth together, refusing to admit that they were a little right about his reluctance to spend time with Edith.

How bad could she be, really? Anyone who loved Nash and was loved by him couldn't be all bad, right? Yet he was afraid of screwing things up or making Edith hate him. If that happened, Nash would have no choice but to take his mother's side, and Cullen could lose the best thing that had ever happened to him.

"Whatever you want to tell yourself to make you feel better." Eric slapped him on the shoulder before he started to walk out. "I'll check your animals, then go and pick Edith up. Do you want me to bring her directly here or should I take her out to your ranch?"

Jeanette snorted. "I think Edith should stay with me. Cullen's ranch isn't fit for a lady. Not at the moment anyway."

Cullen grimaced. "I don't know if it'll ever be fit for a female. It's not like I planned on bringing one home at any point in my life."

"Don't worry. I'll help you out with that and I'm sure

Edith will as well. She'll plan on staying for a while to make sure Nash is healing right."

And the thought of Edith staying for any length of time sent a shiver down Cullen's spine.

"Mr. O'Murphy," the desk nurse called out.

"That's me." He looked at Jeanette. "Are you coming with me?"

Jeanette shook her head. "No. You can handle it from here. I'm going home to set up the guest room for Edith."

She kissed his cheek before leaving. He made his way to where the surgeon stood.

"Mr. Rhodes is out of surgery and in recovery. He's going to be fine."

Chapter Thirteen

Nash heard soft voices talking near him and he wanted to open his eyes to see who happened to be in his bedroom. He couldn't remember who he'd brought home the night before, and the way his head pounded, he might not want to. God knew his judgment tended to be impaired after he'd had a few.

"The doctor said he should be coming around soon," the male voice said.

The man's voice sounded so familiar—like he'd been listening to it all of his life—yet a thought in the back of his mind informed him he might have just met this person. Well, if so, he really wanted to get to know him better.

"I hope so. I need to yell at him for scaring me like this yet again."

He'd recognize that second voice anywhere. His mother was here, and if she had dropped by to visit, why hadn't she told him she was coming? He would've picked her up at the airport.

Wait a minute. She'd said something about scaring her again. What was she talking about? He opened his eyes to stare up at a stark white ceiling. That definitely wasn't his water-stained one in the trailer behind Jeanette's.

Nash turned his head to see his mother looking up at Cullen with a narrow-eyed glare. If Cullen were in his wolf form, he'd have his ears, tail and head down, like Nash's mother had been yelling, "Bad dog," at him.

When he tried to move, a sharp pain tore through his side and he suddenly remembered where he was and why. *Holy fuck! That hurts.* He must have grunted or something because both of them whirled around to face him.

"Nashville, honey, you're okay. The surgeon said you're going to be fine. It'll just take some time to heal up." His mother rushed to his side before taking his hand in hers.

Cullen approached him a little more slowly, and Nash wasn't sure if it was because Mom was here or because he just wasn't sure how to handle the whole thing. Nash held up his other hand and Cullen circled the bed to take hold of him.

He looked at two of the three people he loved most in the entire world. "Are you all right?"

Edith snorted. "How can you ask us that? We're not the ones lying in a hospital bed with four hundred stitches in his side."

Blinking, he asked, "Four hundred?"

"Give or take a stitch. Union got you really good with his knife before I could take him out," Cullen said before he curled his upper lip in a silent snarl.

"It's not your fault. I should've known he wouldn't fight fair and been on the lookout for a knife or gun." Nash squeezed Cullen's hand.

"Still doesn't make me feel better," Cullen mumbled, glancing over at Nash's mother.

"Mom, have you been giving Cullen a hard time about this whole thing?"

Edith looked as innocent as an alligator sneaking up on an unsuspecting meal. "Of course not, honey. Why would I do that? You're a grown man and get into your scrapes without help from anyone."

"Right. I'm sure you remembered that when you punched him."

Cullen looked shocked. "How did you know she hit me?"

"Because she's my mother. She might look little and fragile, but she's really fierce when it comes to her son."

He smiled at his mom. She was petite, only coming to the middle of Cullen's chest. Her hair was still her natural blonde, and it was carefully curled. She wore jeans and a

T-shirt, and Nash couldn't believe she was old enough to be his mother. Of course, she'd had him when she'd been seventeen, so she was younger than most moms with sons his age.

Her brilliant green eyes studied him for a moment. "Do you need anything?"

"We should buzz the nurse so she can let the doctors know you're awake. They'll want to check stuff." Cullen reached for the buzzer with his free hand.

"You're really all right?" Nash had to ask again.

With Cullen being a shifter, he would heal faster than normal humans and, while he looked fine, Nash wanted to make sure his lover hadn't been injured worse than he was saying.

"I'm fine, Nash. Some bruises and scrapes, but nothing time won't heal." After pushing the button, Cullen brushed his fingers over Nash's cheek. "You're the one we were all worried about."

"I thought when you stopped in this one-horse town, you wouldn't get into any more trouble," Edith pointed out.

He shrugged and winced when the movement pulled on his stitches. "It wasn't like I thought Union would follow me or anything, Mom. How was I to know he'd hunt me down? I'm just glad it happened here and not in Santa Monica, where you could've been hurt."

Edith shook her head. "Nashville, you're still recovering from the last beating you took. Couldn't you have waited until the police got there or something? What about those other people you work for?"

Nash saw Cullen stiffen, but he squeezed Cullen's hand again in silent warning. "None of them would've gotten here in time, Mom. Plus, I knew Cullen would be able to deal with them if I couldn't. We were lucky only two of them wanted to fight. Why didn't Hawk join in, and what happened to Union and Rat?"

"Union and Rat are sitting in the sheriff's jail right now, waiting to be returned to Tennessee for their coming trials.

I didn't get involved because I have more pressing issues." Hawk strolled into the room.

Cullen and Edith both growled at the man, bringing a smile to Nash's face. It was good to know he was loved and had people to watch his back when he needed it.

Hawk held up his hands. "Now, I'm one of the good guys."

"Just because you didn't jump into the fight doesn't make you a good guy. It simply makes you a smart one," Cullen pointed out.

"Actually I *am* a good guy, though I couldn't say anything where Union and Rat could hear. I work for the DEA and I've been trying to take Union down for a while now." Hawk looked at Nash. "So good job there, man."

Nash snorted. "Glad to help you out. Do you think you might have said something to me at some point to let me know I wasn't the only spy in the club?"

"No. If you knew, you'd treat me different, and there couldn't be anything that might tip Union off about me...or you, for that matter." Hawk shoved his hands into his back pockets. "I just wanted to let you know the club won't be bothering you anymore. I'm going to take over, and that's all you need to know."

Cullen growled low in his throat, and Nash could tell his lover didn't like how Hawk spoke to him. Nash tugged on Cullen's hand to draw his attention.

"Don't get upset. I don't care how Hawk talks to me. He's right because I don't need to know anything else about the club. I'm not going back to Nashville and I'm not joining another club. I have a different journey to take now."

Cullen stared at him with surprise in his eyes. "Where are you going?"

Nash was aware of his mother drawing Hawk out of the room, but he didn't acknowledge them. It was time to tie his future to the Alpha of the Fallen Creek pack, whether the man wanted it or not.

"Cullen, I love you, and the journey I'm taking next will

be to love you for the rest of our lives. I don't care where that leads me or what I have to do, as long as I get to stay with you." Nash yanked on Cullen's hand, causing Cullen to brace his other one on the bed as he bent over Nash.

After slipping his hand around to the back of Cullen's head, Nash brought their lips together, kissing Cullen with every atom of love he had in him. Cullen whimpered, a sound Nash had never thought he'd hear from the macho Alpha. Cullen opened to him, and Nash nibbled along Cullen's bottom lip.

He didn't want to take the kiss too far since there wasn't any way either one of them could do anything about it at the moment, but he did want Cullen to realize he meant what he said.

It was only when his lungs burned for air that he eased away to rest his forehead against Cullen's. Their breaths mingled as their hearts calmed down and started to beat in time.

"I'm staying here and helping you run the pack. I can keep bartending for Jeanette. I'm pretty sure she won't have a problem with that. You have a Beta in Eric, and we'll see if the two guys I told you about will come as well. The only thing I ask is that we make room for Ten, if he chooses to come out here."

Cullen took a deep breath. "To keep you here, I'll agree to anything. Ten is more than welcome to come and stay with us."

"Good. He's my best friend and he's gone through some really rough times in his life. I want him to know I haven't abandoned him." Nash nuzzled Cullen's cheek. "You'll have to deal with my mother coming to visit us."

"I can handle her visits, Nash, as long as you're with me."

Nash smiled, knowing it was a big deal for Cullen to agree to Edith's coming. For some reason, his mother scared Cullen, and he wasn't sure why.

"Jeanette's going to want to talk to you and your mother at some point," Cullen told him.

"About what?" He let Cullen sit on the edge of the mattress next to him.

"It's not my story to tell, but it'll be an interesting conversation." Cullen rubbed his thumb over Nash's scraped knuckles. "I do love you, Nash, and I appreciate you being willing to change your plans and stay with me."

"What plans? The only plan I had when I left Nashville was to get as far away as possible from Union and the club. When I showed up in Fallen Creek, I had no idea you were here and that I was going to find what I'd been looking for."

"What was that?" Cullen smiled at him, and Nash laughed.

"A grouchy Alpha male who didn't want to save anyone, but ended up saving an entire pack and one half-breed."

Cullen didn't look completely convinced. "Are you sure that was really what you were looking for? Who would really want all of that to deal with? And am I really grouchy?"

Nash laughed. "Just a little, but after you get used to being around people, you should get better."

Grimacing, Cullen shook his head. "I'm not sure that's a selling point, Nash."

Nash had to admit Cullen was right. For a self-proclaimed loner, having to deal with pack members and humans wasn't a reason to be happy. Yet he knew that Cullen would do his job and run the pack the right way, not letting any of them go hungry or get hurt if he could prevent it. The man was nothing if not responsible.

Edith walked into the room. She smiled when she saw the two of them together. "I take it you're not going to be moving out to Santa Monica, Nashville."

He cringed when she said his full name. "No, Mom. I'll be staying here with Cullen. You might like it here. At least once in a while."

"I'd like that. Now we just need to get you healed and out of this hospital."

"Right. Jeanette said you could stay with her in town,

Edith, or you're more than welcome to stay at my ranch. It's not really ready for visitors, but at least it's clean," Cullen informed Edith.

"I appreciate the offer, but I'll stay with Jeanette. It's closer to the hospital, and she said she needed to talk to me about something." Edith reached out and patted Cullen's arm.

Nash smiled at the sight of his lover and his mother slowly building their own friendship. Even though he was in the hospital again, he had to admit that stopping in Fallen Creek had ended up being the best decision of his life.

* * * *

Nash looked up from where he stood by the window in Cullen's living room as Cullen walked in. He'd been released from the hospital two days earlier and had been taking it easy at the ranch. Cullen was doing his best to take care of him, but Nash was getting restless. He thought maybe he'd talk to Jeanette about going back to work.

"Your mom and Jeanette are here," Cullen announced as he sat on the couch, and the ladies entered behind him.

"I thought you weren't coming until tomorrow." He kissed both of them on the cheek before sitting next to Cullen.

"We hadn't planned on it, but we decided we needed to talk to you today. I'm going to fly home tomorrow." Edith patted his cheek. "You're doing fine and Cullen is taking good care of you."

"All right." Nash gestured for her and Jeanette to take a seat. "What do you want to talk about?"

"We've always wondered what kind of shifter you were, right?" Edith said.

"Sure. Once we figured out that there were such things as shifters and I must be one." He leaned against Cullen, who wrapped his arm around Nash's shoulder. "Have you figured out what kind I am?"

"You aren't a shifter, Nash. You're half fae, and that is far rarer than any other creature," Jeanette said.

"Half fae? What does that mean?" He looked at all three of them. "I've never heard of the fae."

"Very few have, or what they have heard are legends because we chose to leave the mortal world long ago, and we've died off to the point there are very few of us left in this world." Jeanette looked sad.

"So you're fae? And my father was as well, but Mom isn't. That's why I could never shift into anything." He glanced over at Cullen with a question in his eyes. "Do you think that's true?"

Cullen shook his head. "I don't know anything about them. I'm not sure if they shift or not. You'd have to talk to Jeanette about that. I'm pretty sure you have a lot of questions to ask her. Good thing you're going to be working at the bar, so you can learn about your heritage."

"Your mother has fae way back in her family tree as well," Jeanette said. "But, yes, from what Edith has told me, I believe your father was fae. One thing I wanted you to know was that, with your mother's permission, I'm going to be looking for your father," Jeanette informed him.

Nash blinked then stared at his mom. "You never told me anything about him, not even when I asked you."

Edith looked down at her hands and sighed before meeting his gaze. "I couldn't talk about him. His leaving me was one of the most painful moments in my life. I never understood what I did wrong."

Jeanette leaned over to pat Edith on her arm. "I've tried to explain to your mother that it wasn't her fault your father left. Fae aren't known for staying in one place for long. We have gypsy souls and tend to wander."

"Whatever you decide, Mom, you know I'll support you," Nash told her, though he was trying to process the whole being fae thing. He'd resigned himself to never knowing what kind of paranormal creature he was, and that he'd never know who his father was. Now he knew half the story, but he still wasn't entirely sure what it meant.

Cullen tightened his grip on Nash's shoulder, and Nash realized it didn't matter what he was. All he really needed to know was who he belonged to, and that was Cullen.

Their hearts might be a little threadbare around the edges, but they'd gotten through the rough parts of living, and, as long as they were together, they could deal with anything the future threw at them.

Voice for the Silent

Excerpt

Chapter One

The cacophony of noise beat Julio down. He kept his gaze averted from the ring, not wanting to see the sickening sight of dogs tearing into each other. The growls, whimpers and yelps were nearly drowned out by the yells of the crowd gathered around the ring. Julio tried to wander through, not pushing or giving any of them a reason to remember him.

The little video camera attached to his shirt captured the faces of the bloodthirsty men and women, though he did notice that most of the women seemed as disgusted with the whole event as he did. They didn't have much say as to whether they wanted to be there or not. Only the dogs had less control than the women over their lives.

Julio hoped the camera caught some good, clear images. It was time to shut down this dog-fighting ring. The men running it were getting suspicious of Julio's constant appearance at the fights, yet he never bet or even stayed the whole night.

His leaving before it was over irritated not only his partner but his superiors. He couldn't tell them that if he stayed until the conclusion, he'd end up vomiting in the corner or something. It was bad enough he went home and took an hour-long shower, trying to wash his body clean of the violence and blood, even when he hadn't gotten close enough to get dirty. His mind imagined him covered in red.

Julio hadn't gotten a full night's sleep since he'd started this assignment, and he doubted he would until it was over. The only light in the whole sordid thing was that he'd gathered enough evidence to shut down this ring, though his boss wanted the smoking gun. He wanted Julio to videotape the men killing underperforming dogs or something equally damning. Julio didn't think he could stay there and watch while a monster killed an innocent dog. It went against everything in his nature.

He'd become a police officer to protect the defenseless, and a Humane Society investigator because, hell, there wasn't anything more defenseless than an animal. They had no voice to speak out against cruelty or abuse. They had no way of sticking up for themselves. Julio could do it for them and wanted to with all of his heart.

His team had shut down three dog-fighting rings so far, but this one was going to be the largest bust in the history of the Humane Society. He would certainly be arresting some of the highest profile people. It would be bigger than when that football player had gotten nailed for running a dog-fighting kennel.

"Hey, Juke," someone spoke from right beside him.

Julio managed not to jump before turning to face Caesar, one of the leaders of the ring. "Hey, man, how's it going?"

"Good, dude. Real good. Got two grand champions set to fight at the end of the night. Oh, I need you to stay after. I got a proposition for you."

Grimacing inside, he nodded. "Cool. I might have to leave for a few but I'll be back."

"Sure. No problem." Caesar squeezed his shoulder hard and wandered off to chat up some other guy wearing an Armani suit.

Who the hell wears Armani to a dog fight?

Julio shook his head and strolled off toward the exit. Tipping his chin to the men guarding the entrance, he slipped out and headed to where his truck sat far enough way from the lights and people that no one could see him pull out his phone.

"What you got, Herendez?"

"Not much except video of the people at the fights, but the big guy wants me to stay after. Says he has a proposition for me."

"You armed?"

"Yeah. They don't expect a dealer like me to wander around without some protection."

"Good. We're not that far away. If something starts going down, you get the hell out of there and we'll take them. I don't want to lose this case, Herendez."

"Understood, sir."

Julio caught movement out of the corner of his eye. "Hey, gotta go. Call you later."

He hung up and stuck his phone in his pocket. Reaching around, he eased the gun from the small of his back and carried it close to his leg, sneaking closer to where the darker shadow was.

"Come on, baby. Just a little farther and you can rest." Desperation colored the speaker's voice.

Julio heard a whimper as he inched closer.

"I know you're hurt. That's why we gotta get you out of there. Uncle will kill you. It don't matter to him that you make good pups. He just sees that you can't fight no more. I won't let you die."

Julio was close enough to see a slender youth leading a limping dog from the back of the building. It was obvious that every step the dog took was painful, but there wasn't any way the kid could carry it. The youth gave the impression that he'd blow away in a gentle breeze. Slender didn't come close to describing the teen. Not sure why he did, Julio disengaged the camera on his shirt. Something said the kid wasn't a willing participant in the fighting.

A twig broke under Julio's foot and the kid dropped, covering the dog with his body. Staring directly at him, Julio thought how incredibly beautiful the kid was. What moonlight drifted through the trees painted the young man's face with silver, highlighting gorgeous cheekbones and illuminating bright blue eyes.

Surprise and fear welled in those eyes, and Julio discovered he wanted to reassure the kid he wouldn't do anything to him. Of course, how believable was that when he held a gun and, if the kid hung around the fights, he'd seen Julio in his undercover role. Juke, drug dealer and all-around badass.

"BB," Caesar shouted, and the kid gasped.

Realizing he was going to regret this, Julio did the only thing his mind would let him get away with. He gestured for the kid to go.

"I got her," he said softly, moving closer to the pair after tucking his gun in his waistband.

"How do I know you won't just shoot her after I leave?"

The kid had guts, Julio gave him that. Not only did he have to worry about Caesar finding out about him taking the dog, but he was questioning Julio like he wasn't carrying a Glock in his waistband and hadn't beat up some asshole for just looking at him wrong.

"You have to trust me, kid. I'll get her out of here." Julio reached out and gave BB a push. "Now go, or he'll come out here and there's no way we'll be able to save her."

"BB, you fucking asshole, where are you? I need you in here." Caesar's voice ripped through the night, causing BB to jerk in terror.

"Go."

Julio didn't wait for BB to move. He swooped in, snatched up the dog, and carried her quickly to his truck. After setting her down, he opened the door and managed to get her in without hurting her worse. At least, he hoped he didn't do any more damage. The dog didn't make a sound, not even growling at him, though she had to be in a lot of pain. Maybe she knew he wouldn't hurt her, or maybe she had lost enough blood, she just didn't care what happened to her.

He stroked her wide head before stepping back and brushing at his shirt. Shit. There were dark streaks on it, which could only be blood. Quickly, he dug through one of his duffel bags and pulled out a clean shirt that was an exact match for the one he wore. After changing them out and switching the camera to the new shirt, he patted the dog one more time and tossed a blanket over her. It would keep her warm. He didn't worry about anyone noticing. The windows were tinted so dark no one could see into the vehicle.

He strolled back inside, nodding to the guard while wandering closer to the ring. There was a lull in the action, and Julio knew it meant the big fight was coming. Two grand champions were slated to fight. One was Caesar's own male, Stu. Julio cringed every time he saw the dog. Stu's face and chest were covered with scars. At times, it seemed like it hurt for Stu to walk or do much of anything, but his overwhelming need to please his owners drove the dog to fight, even when he couldn't move.

The dogs were brought to the ring, and Julio allowed the rush of the crowd to push him out of the way. He'd gotten enough video of the fights, he didn't have to stay around for those. He eased his way through toward the back of the building, where the handlers usually hung around when their dogs weren't fighting. Julio kept his eyes open for BB. Something about the kid called to him.

It had been a long time since Julio had allowed himself to feel any sort of attraction. Yeah, he figured BB was underage—and didn't that make him feel like a perv?—but he couldn't stop thinking about him.

What kind of courage did the kid have that he'd be willing to risk Caesar's wrath by sneaking a wounded dog out of the building? Knowing Caesar as well as Julio did, he wouldn't doubt that if the man discovered the kid doing that, Caesar would kill BB where he stood. No one went against the boss.

The sound of flesh hitting flesh caught his attention, and Julio casually walked down past the cages of dogs. Some of the animals lay quietly, overwhelmed by the scents of fear and anger. Others barked or whimpered, wanting to run away, but trapped in the wire boxes that held them until it was their time for blood and violence.

"I don't want to."

BB's voice drifted to Julio's ear, and he moved closer to one of the remaining stalls in the old barn. It was far enough away from the city not to draw attention, and the owner of the property turned a blind eye to what happened there as long as the money was good.

Staying in the shadows, he peered into the stall and saw Caesar, BB, and another older guy. Blood trickled from a split lip on BB's face, but disgust and more fear shone in the kid's eyes.

"I don't give a shit if you want to or not, BB. This man's paid me good money, so you're gonna do what he wants. You know what'll happen if you don't."

Caesar gestured to the corner where a small brindle pup cowered away from the men. Fuck! Something told Julio threatening the dog would get BB to do anything Caesar wanted.

Defeat settled on BB's shoulders and he pushed away from the corner to walk toward the older guy. Julio didn't like the way the man studied BB, as if the kid was a walking piece of meat he planned on devouring.

None of your business, Julio. You're here for the dogs. Take care of the ring and the kid gets free.

Why didn't that make Julio feel better? His thoughts made him careless and he kicked one of the cages, giving the dog inside a reason to lunge at him.

"Who the hell's there?"

Julio muttered into his phone as Caesar stalked out. He held up a finger at the bald, overweight white man.

"All right, puta. I'll be there in a few minutes. You tell that asshole he don't get nothing until I talk to him. He's screwed me out of too much money."

He flipped his phone shut and punched the wooden stall door in anger. Caesar eyed him suspiciously.

"Sorry, hermano. It sucks being a businessman these days, huh? Can't get good help. They don't stay off the shit." Julio shook his head. "So the fight's about to start. Thought you'd maybe like to watch it with me and give me some pointers on what makes a good fighter. I'm thinking about starting my own kennel."

Caesar stared at him for a moment then broke out into a big smile. "Great idea. I've got a couple pups I could sell you."

Julio glanced over Caesar's shoulder for a quick second, catching BB's questioning gaze. The other man wasn't watching them—he was visually fucking BB where he stood. Julio nodded slightly, knowing BB understood what he was saying, while Caesar thought Julio was agreeing with him.

Some of the tension left BB, but Julio knew BB was still going to have a hell of a night before it was over. He let Caesar drag him off to discuss the finer points of dog-fighting, while Julio tried not to think about what the stranger was doing to BB.

Somehow, he made it through the last fight without losing his mind or the contents of his stomach. When Stu stood, victorious, over his fallen opponent, Julio looked into the dog's eyes and saw no blood lust or rage. No, only anguish and helplessness resided in those dark eyes. This particular dog didn't want to fight. It hadn't been bred into him through centuries of selective genetic manipulation. He'd been trained to fight and knew nothing else, and unfortunately for him, that meant attacking and even killing his fellow canines. Before the handlers closed in, Stu dropped his head and nuzzled the dog, seeming to be saying he was sorry. It broke Julio's heart.

More books from
T.A. Chase

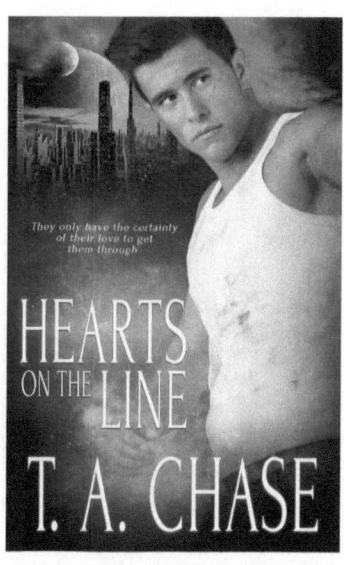

*Baxter and Addison are meant to die, but their love for
each other won't let them choose that future.*

*When an innocent human virgin meets the king of the
unicorn herd, it's not just legends that come true.*

POSSIBILITIES

A roadside meeting during
a hurricane may well lead to
a new relationship.

T. A. CHASE

When Dixon and Carson meet during a hurricane, neither imagined that moment would be the beginning of a new relationship.

A man looking for revenge discovers a man who wants to save a city.

About the Author

T.A. Chase

There is beauty in every kind of love, so why not live a life without boundaries? Experiencing everything the world offers fascinates TA and writing about the things that make each of us unique is how she shares those insights. When not writing, TA's watching movies, reading and living life to the fullest.

T.A. Chase loves to hear from readers. You can find contact information, website details and an author profile page at https://www.pride-publishing.com/